The
Black Lamp

Bread-taxed weaver, all can see
What that tax hath done for thee.
        E. Elliott: *Corn Law Rhymes.*

PETER CARTER

The Black Lamp

ILLUSTRATED BY DAVID HARRIS

London
OXFORD UNIVERSITY PRESS
1973

Oxford University Press, Ely House, London W.1
GLASGOW NEW YORK TORONTO MELBOURNE WELLINGTON
CAPE TOWN IBADAN NAIROBI DAR ES SALAAM LUSAKA ADDIS ABABA
DELHI BOMBAY CALCUTTA MADRAS KARACHI LAHORE DACCA
KUALA LUMPUR SINGAPORE HONG KONG TOKYO

ISBN 0 19 271356 6

© Peter Carter 1973

First published 1973

*All rights reserved. No part of this publication may be reproduced,
stored in a retrieval system, or transmitted, in any form or by any means,
electronic, mechanical, photocopying, recording or otherwise, without
the prior permission of Oxford University Press*

Text set in 11/12 pt. Monotype Baskerville, printed by photolithography,
and bound in Great Britain at The Pitman Press, Bath

CHAPTER ONE

I was born in the village of Helmshaw in the vale of Rossendale, in Lancashire, in the year 1803, when our country was at war with the armies of the French Republic. A soldier's scarlet coat was then a sign of glory and 'King and Country' was all the Patriots' cry, but still there were those, like my father, who asked, 'Whose king and whose country?' and who thought that the 'Ça Ira' was as good a tune as any they had heard.

My father's name was George Cregg. He was named for a king, but myself he called Daniel, after that hero of the Hebrews who went into a lions' den for his beliefs. My mother died giving birth to my sister, Emma. I was but five years old then and so I scarcely remember her. She is buried under a slab of millstone in Haslingden churchyard and, when I can, I go there and place a sprig of flowers on her grave.

Because of my mother's death my father had to be both mother and father to me and I, in turn, had to be both brother and mother to Emma. Had my father been in any other trade he would have had to marry again, but he was a hand-weaver and they, you must know, do their work at home, and so our father could earn our bread and watch over us as well.

I say that my father was a weaver and he was a good one. He was a Jacquard weaver and had a special loom with cards with holes in them to weave the fine patterns of the fancy stuff. The cards hung over the loom and every draught set them swaying. On a hot day it was pleasant to hear them rustle like leaves on a tree. As well as being a good weaver, father was one wise in his generation, for he could read well and write a little. He placed great value on learning and at an early age he sent me down to

Waterfoot where an old dame called Mother Seddon kept a school. There I, too, learned to read and write, do arithmetic to the Rule of Three, and I was taught the names of birds and flowers, and the Five Continents and the Seven Seas, and all for threepence a week.

The clack of the loom I can hear now in my imagination. At the beginning of the week it had a slow, pleasant sound: 'plenty of time, plenty of time'; but as market day drew near, it changed its tune. 'Hurry it up, a day too late, hurry it up, a day too late' was its cry then, for if the cloth was not ready the clothier might refuse it, although that was rare in those days. The wars against the French meant a great demand for cloth. Every soldier needed his red coat, every sailor his blue jacket; and the Government spent money as though, like King Midas, they had but to touch the dirt of the ground for it to turn into gold.

Our village was small but I would not have you think that it was dull. We had an inn, the Robin Hood, and in those prosperous days, when weavers could buy books as well as beer, we had clubs which used to meet there and discuss the affairs of the day. The turnpike from Bury to Blackburn ran under our noses and there were always people passing along it. It might be a ragged beggar, his face white with hunger under a sunburn, or a soldier tramping off to join his regiment; or a gang of Irishmen, looking for rough work, who always seemed to be laughing and joking in their strange language, which none but they understood. Sometimes a squadron of the Yeoman Cavalry came trotting past in their gaudy uniforms and, every week, the sturdy weavers of the moorland parishes tramped past with their lengths of cloth on their way to market. And, one day, something went by which I did not then fully understand.

I was, perhaps, nine or ten at the time. It was a day in Spring, but not a fine one. The weather was cold and sleety. There was still snow on the hills and the lambing was late. Father woke us early and, when we had dressed and had our gruel and tea, told us to go down into the valley and fetch white may-blossom, as much as we could gather. We ran down to the woods, filled our arms with blossom, and carried it back to our house. Father took it from us and walked out, down to the Robin Hood. Many people were gathered there and I wondered why they had come together on a working day. When they took the may and put it in their coats and hats I wondered more, for it was not the custom in Helmshaw.

The folk lounged about by the inn but in a queer way. They did not talk but moved restlessly, as I have seen birds in flocks move when they think an enemy near; first one and then another lifting its head and fluttering uneasily for a yard or two before settling again. It was strange to see the men move so, and stranger still to see them decked with the may, which looked dazzling white against their drab clothes.

As I was wondering about this I heard the jingle of harness and a troop of dragoons entered the village. They were led by an officer, stiff in red and gold, who, when he saw the people gathered, trotted forward with a hard-looking sergeant by his side. The officer stood in his stirrups and looked down on the people.

'Who is the leader here?' he asked.

On hearing this, the crowd gave a sullen growl. One of the weavers spat at the horse's hooves.

'We have no leaders,' he said. 'We are free men here.'

The officer scowled at him. 'I wish for no trouble today,' he cried in a harsh voice.

'Neither do we,' said my father. 'But we have the right to stand by our inn if we choose.'

The officer looked around a little helplessly when he heard this and shrugged his shoulders. 'Very well. But if there is any disturbance, I warn you, I will put the troops on you.'

With that he waved the soldiers forward. They formed a scarlet rank against the people, and got black looks for their trouble. But still the crowd was quiet. Then we heard more horses and a heavy coach rumbled from the mist. There were soldiers with it and some gentlemen, one in the uniform of the Yeomanry. As the coach drew into the village there was a storm of booing from the crowd. Inside the coach there was a flurry of movement and a man thrust his hands through the window. I heard the clank of iron and saw that he was manacled. He gave a cry. What it was I do not know for a guard seized him and dragged him down. The crowd shook with anger at that. They booed and shouted again. The dragoons clapped their hands on their sabres and pushed their horses forward, driving the people back. Then someone gave a wild cry and shouted, 'Ludd will free thee!'

One of the gentlemen, he in the Yeomanry uniform, swung his head around sharply when he heard that. He spurred his horse forward. 'Who shouted?' he demanded. 'What villain called that name?'

There was no answer. Behind the red fence of the soldiers the people stared at him in a sullen silence. The gentleman cursed.

'Why do you wear those favours?' he demanded, meaning the may which everyone wore.

James Adshead, who was a tall, strong weaver, and my father's best friend, spoke up then. 'They are not favours, they are flowers.'

'Aye, and all white!' the gentleman roared. 'Do you think that I do not know what that colour means, or why you wear it? It is the colour of treason and rebellion. You are a pack of damned Radicals. Take them off!'

He glared around at the crowd. 'Do you hear me? Take them off, I say.' And he raised his whip as if to strike at James.

My father stepped forward then. 'If we wish to wear flowers then we will do so. Or will you have us cut down for that?'

The gentleman went crimson with rage. 'Dare you speak to me so?' he bellowed. 'I am Colonel Fletcher, and I am the Chief Magistrate of Bolton.'

Father looked up at the Colonel and smiled. 'Be you so?' he asked coolly. 'Well, I am George Cregg, and I am the Secretary of the Botanical Club of Helmshaw.'

The crowd roared with laughter at that but the Colonel set his teeth with rage. 'I know your type, and your clubs. You are a pack of seditious traitors.'

And then he called my father an insolent, villainous dog. There might well have been bloodshed for that but another gentleman drew the Colonel away. He urged him forward and waved the coach on, and the dragoons, who seemed glad to be rid of their task, splashed after it. As they left the village, there was a general groan of derision and someone called out, 'Liberty!' Then the coach, and the gentlemen, and the soldiers, were gone.

Some of the men stayed talking and some went in the Robin Hood, but my father walked off home. I ran after him and asked him who the men in the coach were and why the troops had been in our village. For a time he would not answer me but, at last, he burst out in a bitter voice.

'Those men are being taken to Lancaster to be hanged. They are weavers from Bolton. There are machines there which will make cloth cheaper than a weaver can. They saw the work being taken from their hands and the bread being taken from their mouths and so they broke the machines. They took desperate measures, and now they are to pay a desperate price. We gathered to bid them farewell. We ought to have . . . '

He stared at his hands for a while and whispered, as if to himself, 'We let them go to their hanging with scarcely a word.'

Not much of this I understood. Towns like Bolton, and the goings-on there, were nearly as strange to me as China. But I asked who that man might be who was to free the prisoners; that Ludd whose name had been called out.

My father shook his head. 'He is a man who does not exist. A name without a being. Think no more of him.'

With that he rose and went out, down to the Robin Hood, which was a thing he did rarely during the day, and I saw no more of him until he came in tipsy and fell asleep before the fire.

CHAPTER TWO

The events of that day disturbed me deeply. The rattle of a catch on a door, or the chain on a dog, was enough to bring back the memory of hands thrusting through a coach window. At night I dreamed of the mysterious Ludd, that man without existence, that name without a being. And I dreamed, often enough, of the gallows at Lancaster.

More than one coach rumbled through our village after that day. In the towns, in Bury and Bolton and Manchester, the workmen saw the new machines coming in and they did not like what they saw. Every new machine was a threat to them, for, if one machine did the work of five men, what became of those men? And so they rose and broke the machines. But each time they rose the soldiers came and drove them down—and that with sabres and guns.

The troops were everywhere in those days. They say that there were more soldiers in the North than Wellington took to the Peninsula, and it was easy to believe. Wherever you went, it was not long before you heard the jingle of harness and the clopping of horses' hooves, and we grew used to the sight of scarlet on our grey-green hills.

For a time it was like living in an occupied country for there was no love lost between us and the troops. Even on the moors, where we were independent men, owning our own looms, we hated the soldiers. There is nothing which irks a man more than to see the Cavalry galloping past, careless of the cloth stretched on the tenter frames, especially when he fears that it might be his turn next to feel the sabre across his back. A sullen lot the troops were too. Why, it was easy to see. Every weaver's hand was against them, and so their hand was against every weaver.

We children were forbidden to speak to the soldiers, or any strangers whatever. Of course this was because we might echo our parents' hostility to the troops and they find themselves hauled before the magistrates, charged with helping the machine-breakers. This led to strange happenings. We might be playing on the road and some harmless stranger come along only to see the pack of us take to our heels as if he bore the plague and, if he lingered, find himself bombarded with stones.

Because of this we found ourselves living in an isolated world. Although we knew that great events were taking place about us, we did not know for sure what they were. Not a man among those we knew would utter a word. It was as if all the people of the North had agreed upon a great oath of secrecy—and well they knew how to keep it. But despite this we heard whispers—echoes almost—of what was happening among our hills. Especially we heard the name Ludd!

Our picture of him was a garbled one, to be sure. We heard that he was a general and that he lived in Shirewood Forest with a band of outlaw weavers. At night he came from the forest seeking out bad master-clothiers who had put machines in their shops and, if he found one, first breaking his bones, then his machines, then burning down the roof over his head. I had a picture of a great hairy boggart with burning eyes, like Jinny Greenteeth, striding across moor and vale as though he wore ten-league boots. I thought of him as a creature half-friend, half-foe, for it was not beyond belief that Ludd might make a mistake and, seeing me, think that if I were not a hard master then I might be a hard master's son! So, for a while, I went carefully and made sure that I was in our house when night fell.

But there were good times and bad in the weaving trade. The country was mad for cloth and no loom needed to stay idle. The machines were spinning thread by the mile and the clothiers had to find men to weave it, and they were ready to pay good money to any man who would. When these better times came along, the weavers settled down for a while and stopped their rioting, the soldiers went back to their quarters and, little by little, Ludd faded from our memories.

Freed from Ludd, I turned to my own interests again. These were simple enough. I liked trees and running water, birds' nests and frogs. I liked running and fighting, frightening girls and making weird noises. Reading pleased me too. The Old Dame had a Bible which I went through from cover to cover. A great deal of it I did not follow but I liked the battles, and the names. These I would chant on my way to school: Og and Basan, Bezalel and Zadok, David and Jonathan. At home we had *Gulliver's Travels*, *The Pilgrim's Progress*, *The Merchant of Venice*, by William Shakespeare, and Tom Paine's *The Rights of Man*, although I must confess that these last were too hard for me to read. As well as these, we had toy books in plenty which father brought home for us on market day. I taught Emma her letters from Mother Goose's Toy Book. She was ever a gentle, obedient child and she sat by me at the spinning wheel as good as gold, chanting away:

> 'A is an Archer who shot at a frog,
> B was a butcher who had a great dog . . .'

But although I liked reading well enough, most of all I liked to roam the wild moors. There was a hamlet up there called Heytop. In it lived a tribe of Methodist Ranters. On fine evenings they used to gather on their moor and listen to their leader, a lame fustian weaver whose name was Briggs but who called himself Brother Obadiah. It was a queer sight to see the Ranters gathered around him, screeching their gory hymns, confessing their sins, and falling down in dead faints. We lads of Helmshaw would sit on the wall and screech too, but with mirth rather than repentance, for we were true weavers' sons and cared little for the wrath of Jehovah and nothing at all for the wrath of Brother Obadiah.

I have often thought about our boldness for there is little of it to be seen now-a-days, and the thought comes to me that we were bold because our fathers were, we were independent because they were, and we had good food in our bellies and stout broadcloth on our backs.

But there was one place where we were neither bold nor independent. Nearby there was a little wooded valley, or clough, as they are called in Lancashire. In this clough, which was called

Fenner's Clough, after a murderer who had lived there and who had been hanged on a gibbet at the cross-roads, a worse villain named Cranley came and built a mill for the spinning of thread. We could not see the mill from our moor for it was lost to sight in the Clough, but we were ever conscious that it was there. On still days we could hear the clatter of the water-wheel as it thrashed round and we could hear the thud, thud, thud, of the machines as they meshed out the thread. At night, too, we could see beams of light shining from the dark chasm and, worst of all to us children, if, daring greatly, we ran to the top of the Clough and peered through the thickets of oak and ash, we could sometimes see the children who worked there.

They were mainly orphan paupers apprenticed—at least that was what it was called—by Parishes as far away as London who wished to be free from the burden of feeding them. My father, and he was not alone, said that it was worse than slavery and that Cranley and the Parishes were no better than the merchants of Liverpool who bought and sold blackamoors. It was the great fear of our lives that one day we too might be sent down into the Clough, to be bound at the mill, to join the ghosts of Fenner's victims, and the more piteous shades in Cranley's mill.

CHAPTER THREE

Cranley himself we often saw for he lived in a house he had built in the mill. He was a raw, coarse brute, built like a bull-dog with stumpy legs and a flat face, mottled red and white, slit by a harsh mouth. He always had a dog with him. It was a savage thing, as evil looking as its owner. That it had no name tells something about Cranley, I think.

Cranley was forever smoking a pipe and when I think of him I remember that pipe, and the long plume of black smoke that rose from it wreathing his tall black hat. They were, it seems to me, symbolic of the days to come, when the tall factory chimneys were to rise in our green valleys and their smoke was to hang over us all.

He used to jog through our village on a horse as shabby and unkempt as its rider—I will say this for him: although a rich man, he never altered his speech nor his dress but stayed the same rough fellow he had been when he first came to Helmshaw, and that whether he was strutting about his mill or riding with the gentry of Bolton when they played at being soldiers in the Yeomanry.

He had been many things in his time: a sailor, a navigator, a ganger on the building of the new docks at Liverpool, and a weaver himself. But where he had got his money from no one could say for sure. There were many stories told. That they were all evil says as much about Cranley as about the scandal loving tale-tellers who told them, for he was the sort of man around whom such tales gather as, they say, flies in dark clouds swarm around gypsies.

Our village had little to do with Cranley. He spun his thread, gave it out to hand-weavers to be made up into cloth, and took it back for the finishing bit, but none of our weavers ever worked for him. Most of them could afford to buy their own yarn from the clothiers in Haslingden or Bury or Rochdale, and they took it there to be finished. They saw no need to turn to a sullen dog like Cranley. Besides which he only spun for the coarsest fustians and most of us were a cut above that, making good broadcloth and worsted. As for father, he sold his cloth in Bolton where there was a market for the fine stuffs he wove.

If I, or the other village lads, saw Cranley we kept clear. This was not just because we feared his dog but because of something about the man himself. Even the boldest of us never shied a lump of turf at his tall hat. This fear of him was, I think, mixed in our minds with fear of his mill and the whimpering things that cried there at the jennies. We had, indeed, something of the fear and awe for Cranley that we had for the Devil and his dark kingdom. Then, one day, he spoke to me.

It happened in the autumn, on a bleak, blustery day, with a sharp wind coming off the hills and spats of rain in the air. With Emma, I was wandering along the turnpike in the way that children do, poking into every cranny of the walls and squelching through the slutch of the ditch looking for frogs. I heard the sound of a horse and, looking behind me, I saw Cranley coming. I took Emma by the hand and we ran off. I was partly afraid and partly making believe, as though Cranley might be the Giant Appolyon, or Bloody-Man, who would devour us if he should catch us.

We had not gone above ten yards when I heard Emma cry out. I turned to see Cranley's dog slashing at her dress. No matter what I felt for its master I had no fear of the dog and I kicked it in the head. I wore clogs banded with iron. A blow from them would have driven off a mastiff and the dog backed away, still snarling and slavering, but shaking its head in a way that was almost comical.

Then Cranley rode up, not hurrying, and stared down at us from his saddle.

'You are not feared of the dog, then?' he asked, in a sneering sort of way.

'Not I,' I shouted boldly.

Cranley gave a sort of grin—his mouth split a little showing some splintered, black stumps of teeth.

'If I set him on you he would tear you to ribbons,' he said.

'Try it!' I cried, and shoved Emma behind me, ready to face the brute again.

Cranley laughed at me but said no more and turned away. I watched him angrily and when I turned and saw Emma in tears my anger flared into rancour. I took a step forward and shouted after him, 'Ludd will get you—and your dog!'

Why I shouted that I hardly knew myself. It was merely an echo of the words that I had heard years ago when the machine-breakers were taken through our village, words which meant little enough to me. But at the sound of them Cranley stopped dead. For a moment he sat motionless, then he turned his flat, evil face around and stared at me. For a long moment he looked at me like that and then he turned his horse and came back to me. Again he looked down at me but this time there was no cracking of his face in a laugh, no matter how evil that laugh might be.

'Where did you hear that name?' he demanded, and when I did not speak he leaned down so that his face was close to mine.

'Where did you hear that name?' he asked again.

I did not answer for I was numb with fear, and indeed there was that expression on Cranley's face which would have frightened a grown man, let alone a lad of my years. After a moment Cranley straightened in his saddle and moved off.

I quieted Emma and we went on to our house. When we got there I saw Cranley at the door talking to my father. I had no wish to see the mill-owner again so I slipped in through the back-door. I lingered in the scullery for a minute until Cranley cleared off then went into the front room. Father stood at the door for a while before coming in and sitting at his loom. He set to work, now and then throwing a glance at me, but saying nothing.

I was uneasy for I thought that Cranley might have laid some lying complaint against me. Of Ludd I thought nothing at all. However I kept my mouth shut and waited for my father to speak. Finally he turned from the loom.

'You are a growing lad,' he said, 'and a strong one, too.'

That pleased me, of course. Like all lads I wished for nothing better than to be a man.

'Aye, you are a big lad,' father continued, 'I think it time that you earned your living.'

I jumped up at that, delighted, and was ready to run into Bolton for another loom on the instant. Father rose too and put his coat on. He took Emma by the hand and bid me follow him. The three of us strolled down the village street and onto the moor. There we lay in the heather and gazed across the valley.

'See you,' father said, and pointed across the vale. There, where a stream ran briskly in a clough, we could see a mill abuilding.

'There are four mills in this valley already,' said father, 'and that will make five. The machine-breakers did not stop them coming and I doubt now that anything will.' He looked sombre.

'I think the day of the hand-weaver is coming to an end, Daniel.'

That I could not follow. How could the weavers come to an end? Were men to stop wearing cloth?

Father shook his head.

'It is not that, but look at the spinning mills. One of them can spin more thread in a day than you and Emma in a year, though you worked day and night. Who would have ever thought that? And now there are machines that can weave coarse stuff. If so be they make them that they can weave fine cloth, what will happen to the weaver then? Where will a man be?'

For my part I could not believe this. That a machine could weave the delicate thread into warp and weft seemed as strange as that men might walk on the moon. But father was stubborn.

'Men said that about the spinning until Crompton and Arkwright came along, and now how many jennies are there?' He stared across the vale as if he could see a vision there, like the prophets in the Bible.

'I see it happening. Black times are coming for the weavers, black times.'

He shook his head as if awakening from a trance.

'No,' he said. 'I will put you to another trade.'

So saying he walked us home. And the next day he was as good as his word, for he took me by the hand and walked me through the village and down to Fenner's Clough, and put me to work in Cranley's mill.

CHAPTER FOUR

My father took me by the hand and walked me down into the Clough and set me to work in Cranley's mill. And as we walked there I wondered how he could so betray me and take me to such a place—one that he had cursed often enough; where the children flitted through the gloom like ghosts, their faces wetter than the water-wheel with salt tears.

But although he led me by the hand through the thickets of oak and ash, and into the darkness, I did not go as a slave to the jenny. Instead I went into the room where the millwright laboured and was set to work learning the mysteries of the engineering trade.

I often wondered why Cranley should have chosen me to be a workman in his mill, for there was no love lost between him and my father. In my innocence I thought that I had been picked because I was strong and active, and because I could read and write and do my sums, as a good engineer must. I quite forgot that I had taunted Cranley with the name of Ludd. But for that I think I might be forgiven, as I was only twelve years of age.

My master in the mill was the mechanical worker, whose name was Bloom. He was a tall man, although much bent by leaning over his work-bench. He had slaty eyes and a yellowish skin, which is common among engineers for they spend little time in the open air. When I first met him I thought he was from some such barbarous part as the old dame had spoken of, for, beside his strange eyes and yellow skin, he spoke in the queerest way, saying 'poipes' for pipes, 'loike' for like, 'oi' for I, and so on. But I soon found out that this was because he was from

Birmingham Town, where they all speak in such a strange way but which is famous for its machines.

In Birmingham, which Bloom called Brummigum, he had worked at the manufactory of Boulton and Watt which, as all engineers know, is the best place in the world for machines and

engines. Bloom was very proud of having worked there. Watt and B. he called it when he spoke, which was seldom, for he was a silent man and when he wished for anything he usually pointed with his long yellow finger. But for all his tawny skin and outlandish speech, he was not a bad man. He often gave the pauper children a scrap of bread dipped in treacle, and when he saw them being whipped by the overseer—a brute named Burns—he would say to me that it was a 'croying shame'.

For my part I was not of those years which might have enabled me to feel the pity for the children which I should, perhaps, have done. Indeed, for a time I was too sorry for myself to spare any grief for others. My worst fears were quieted when I found that I was to go home every night; but at first I felt like a prisoner inside the stone walls, and the sound of the machinery was a great torment to me, for it never varied or stopped; hour after hour it persisted, 'Clack, thrash, clack; clack, thrash, clack'. My head was pained all day with that sound and I took it home with me, where it pursued me into my dreams.

But I grew used to the noise and I found things in the mill I liked doing. I enjoyed cutting the black iron and bending it into strange shapes, and I liked standing by the forge blowing the fire into a white heat while Bloom hammered metal on the anvil, sending sparks of golden fire across the work-shop. I even liked going into the mill when a machine had broken down, which they often did, and watching Bloom creep under it, tapping and scraping and knocking until he came out and said, 'It's all roight neuw,' by which he meant that it was all right now. Sometimes he made me laugh, for whatever the machine was like he would shake his head and say that it was no good at all. This was because the machines came from Preston, and whatever had not come from Watt and B. was damned in his eyes. The truth of the matter was that I preferred working in the mill to weaving, and it gave me a heavy conscience at times, making me feel like a traitor to my father.

Our machines were run by water-power. At the head of the Clough Cranley had dammed the brook. Where the brook ran from the dam there was a wooden gate called a sluice, and this could be opened or closed to control the flow of water to the mill. In dry, summer weather, the stream which drove the water-wheel sometimes failed and became no more than little pools, and in the winter it might freeze over. When either of these things happened the wheel slowed and the jennies nodded backwards and forwards as idly as old women falling asleep in a rocking chair. Then Bloom would point with his yellow finger and it was my task to scramble up the Clough and open the sluice.

The way up there was not easy. The path ran alongside a cleft in the rocks, where ferns sprouted in the summer and icicles in the winter, and it would have been easy to slip down into it and be killed. But going up there was the job I liked most of all. It took me away from the mill walls and set me free among the woods. I kept a sharp look-out for ghosts, you may be sure, but I was bold enough for them in the day-time.

At the dam I had to walk out along a wall to the sluice wheel and haul it around until the gate opened. As it lifted, the water ran out from under it, sleek and gentle, but as the gap widened it spouted into the chasm below and roared and thundered among the rocks. Then the wheel began to groan as it was forced around and the jennies began to clatter, as if the old women had woken up and fallen to prattling.

The water-wheel I liked very much. It had not the same monotonous sound as the machines. Although it made a huge noise, its voice was endlessly varied as it went round and round and the water gushing through its great paddles had a pleasant gurgle which put me in mind of days fishing in the Irwell. It had, too, a thing which I did not fully recognise then. Although the sluice could keep it working at our command, it had a natural rhythm, a slowing down or speeding up, which made it possible to feel, in a dim way, a link between oneself and the world outside: with streams and rain and clouds and sunshine.

One day when I was at the sluice I noticed marks on the timbers. They were white slashes against the slimy green of the woodwork and looked to have been made by an axe. When I got back to the mill I mentioned this to Bloom and he hastened to tell Cranley. Nothing would do then but that the three of us must go up to the sluice and see them. Cranley and Bloom were perturbed about the marks.

'Someone has been trying to destroy the sluice,' Bloom said, and shook his solemn head.

Cranley was less solemn and much more savage. He vowed that Bloom was right.

'It is one of them damned weavers,' he bellowed. 'I will have a guard put on up here. If I catch the villain he will regret having attacked my property.'

'It is a mortal business,' Bloom agreed. 'Whoever did it could find himself on the gallows.'

Cranley twisted his ugly face. 'It won't be the gallows he finds himself on. I will throw him down the Clough.'

It was an ugly threat but Cranley was an ugly enough person to carry it out. After that, nothing would satisfy Cranley but that I should go up the Clough a dozen times a day—which pleased me. At night there had to be a guard. Bloom flatly refused to be this and, as it was impossible for me to be given the task, it fell to Burns to do it. It pleased me to think of the overseer cowering by the dam while I lay snug in my bed and I took the whole thing with a light heart. Bloom, though, was more serious.

'If the timbers up there were weakened, and if there was a full dam, the sluice could burst and the waters would carry away the whole mill.' And he frowned at me, not for taking lightly the threat to ourselves, but for failing to show proper concern for his precious machines.

I told my father about the attack on the sluice. He listened impassively, but when I told him that I had run to the master with the news he gave me a curious glance out of the corner of his eye, a rather calculating look; the sort a man might give another if judging whether he is a rogue or a fool. But though the attack led to that cold look from my father, it also led to Cranley speaking to me.

Of course Cranley had spoken to me before, but that was mainly in the way of orders and in a tone the same as he used to his dog. On this day, though, he called me over to him in a way which was almost human. He complimented me on finding the axe-marks on the sluice and went so far as to give an imitation of a smile. I did not know how to respond to this. Pleasant words from Cranley seemed as unnatural as tears from a statue. Besides which his manner, even when he was trying to charm, was so gross that it was hard not to feel disgusted in his company.

After he had spoken I started to move away, but Cranley seemed inclined to chatter.

'How is your father, lad?' he asked.

'Well enough,' I said, wondering why Cranley should ask, for he did not care two farthings for anyone but himself.

'Aye,' said Cranley, 'I am glad to hear it. Glad to hear it,' he repeated, as if trying to convince himself of the truth of this.

'He has settled down well here. I am glad of it. Once a man starts to wander it is a hard thing for him to stay still. Your Dad has travelled, I believe?'

I mumbled assent to this. Cranley gave me an oily grin.

'Now I have been a traveller myself and I am interested in where other men have been. Where might your father have journeyed to? I would be interested in knowing that.'

I might have answered Cranley, for I knew that my father had lived in Spen Valley in Yorkshire, but as I opened my mouth Cranley opened his and spat out a stream of tobacco-stained phlegm. Seeing that dirty action while my father's name was on his lips disgusted me and I could not bring myself to answer him. Instead I shrugged the question off, saying that I did not know where my father had been. Cranley's amiable manner disappeared in an instant and he ordered me back to work.

Following that I saw little of Cranley for he was away a good deal. He had begun to spend much of his time in Bury, where the manufacturers of the town had become political under the leadership of Robert Peel, the greatest mill-owner in the County. He was also hand-in-glove with Colonel Fletcher of Bolton and they planned to build a big new mill which would be run not by water—but by steam!

This pleased Bloom and did that which I had thought nothing on earth would do—made him talk! When he first heard of Cranley's plans he came into our workshop rubbing his hands with glee.

'Steam!' he cried. 'Steam! Now we shall see something. Now we shall wake up! No more of that—' he waved at the waterwheel. 'We shall have steam, and coal, and engines. Something a man can work at. And all made by Watt and B.' And at that name his eyes glittered, as if he was the faithful pilgrim Christian, seeing the Celestial City.

I was as excited as Bloom by this. Visions came into my head of great shining cylinders and gleaming pumps, all made of iron and brass and copper, with a roaring fire beneath and Bloom stooping before it like Ahab the Ishmaelite before the idol of Baal. But there was more to come:

'They are going to build a canal as well. Why, when that comes there will be dozens of mills in the valley. Think of that—why, it will be better than Brummigum!'

I ran home that night anxious to tell my father the news. It was a sharp night and the rain slashed at the windows and the wind whined down the chimney as I told of the coming of the steam-engines and the canals. Father was interested despite himself, but when I had finished he shook his head.

'It will be a new power in the land, but whose hands will control it save that dog Cranley and his like? What does the coming of these new things mean to the likes of me? Rich men will come into this vale and prance about, but they will do us no good.'

He rose from the loom and fretted for a moment by the fire. Then he bade Emma, who was staring into the flames, to get to her bed. When she was gone he turned to me. He told me of how the rich men in the Kingdom ruled the roost and that the poor men, be there never so many of them, had no say in the affairs of the country. He told me of the Government in London that ruled us all, and of the Parliament there where the great Lords lolled and allowed no one to give them the nay to their desires.

'But why should men like Liverpool and Castlereagh sit there and not the likes of me? Look at this vale. The man who represents it in the Parliament is the son of the Duke of Devonshire. I have never set eyes on him in my life—nor he on me—yet he passes laws which strike at my very living.'

As he said this my father's face grew bitter, for he was not one to take easily to being told what he must do by anyone, whether they lived far away or in the same parish.

'Aye,' he said. 'Such men talk of freedom but they mean the freedom to put their heels on my neck. Men have been sent to the scaffold for daring to ask why this should be. Cobbett and Tom Paine had to flee the country because they asked, and I have known men transported for life because they whistled a French tune and made a few idle boasts when they were drunk. No, I do not wish rich men near me. They bring with them rich men's laws—and I have tasted enough of them.'

I listened and began to grasp what he was saying. Before then I had heard things said against the government, but I had cared little for such talk. Now I began to feel as angry as my father. And then, as wrath began to rise within me at the thought that there should be men who could rule over us, there came a knock at the door. It was not a hard knock but a tap more like, as if the tapper knew that there would be those inside waiting and listening for the tap.

'Who might that be?' I asked, and made for the door, but father held out his hand.

I stopped, and then again came the tap, three times quick, twice slow, and then again three times quick.

'Stay you still,' ordered my father, and he went to the door and opened it, but not wide, merely a crack.

From the darkness came a voice.

'Brother George?' it asked.

At that I nearly burst out laughing, thinking that whoever was outside had mistaken us for the Ranters on the moors who called everyone 'Brother'. But to my surprise, my father answered:

'I might be; they say all men are brothers. Who might you be?'

'Brother John,' the voice said, and then, softly, but not so soft that I did not catch it, 'The grip's on'.

My father's back stiffened.

'And will it hold?' he asked.

''Twill hold forever,' answered the voice, and then my father opened the door and two strangers came into our house.

CHAPTER FIVE

The door opened and the wind set the pattern-cards over the loom swaying and rustling. I stayed still in my corner as I had been bidden and in the uncertain light the strangers did not catch sight of me. I, though, had a good look at them. One of them was a big, strong fellow with a hard, scarred face. He was not the sort of man you would wish for an enemy. The other man was smaller, not strong looking, and with teeth sticking out like a rabbit. As they entered, father backed into the room, almost as if he was afraid of them. I did not like to see that.

The big man faced my father and held up his hand in a strange way, with his thumb crossed over the palm and his little finger bent down.

'You will remember that sign,' he said, and then he caught sight of me. He whipped around like a top and his face went as white as though he saw Old Nick himself sitting by the fire.

'What's this?' he cried, and his voice shook—with rage I thought then, although I know now that it was fright.

Father put his hand on my shoulder. 'No need to fear,' he said. 'This is my son, Daniel.'

The stranger took a gulp of air. 'Is he twisted in?' he asked.

Father stared steadily at the stranger.

'Twisted in,' he repeated. 'I had thought never to hear those words again.' Then he gave his head a little shake, which was a trick he had when about to fall into a musing state.

'No, the lad is not twisted in.'

'Then send him out.' The great man waved a fist as big as my head.

Father hesitated, but not for long.

'No, there will be nothing said tonight that he may not hear. The days of that sign you gave are long past. The boy will stay, but he will get you food if you desire, and your friend too.'

Brother John looked at me shrewdly, then at my father and shrugged.

'So the Black Lamp is out, eh?'

'Out for ever,' father answered.

'Well, well.' There was something taunting in John's voice but he did not argue. 'We would be glad of a bite to eat if you have anything to share.'

I did not wait for orders but rushed into the scullery, snatched up bread and cheese, and dashed back into the front room. My father and John were sitting by the fire. The other man had taken a seat on the loom-bench where he was half hidden by shadow. They took the food and ate, John biting off huge mouthfuls and washing them down with weak ale. When they had finished my father spoke.

'Now, come to your business. But no gallows talk here.'

At that my heart knocked against my ribs and I held my hand before my mouth. What talk could that be which might lead us to the gallows? At the sound of the word I felt a hatred for the strangers who had brought it into our house. But my father looked calm and at ease as he lounged in his chair and seeing him like that eased my fears.

John waved his fist.

'Nothing of that, no gallows talk. We travel all legal and would have been here in broad daylight but bad weather held us up on the moors. We have come from Yorkshire. 'Twas there that we got your address.'

As he spoke he peered closely at my father as if he expected him to show some emotion, but father kept a composed face.

'I am known among the weavers there as I am here,' he said.

'As you say.' John wagged his head as if this satisfied him. 'We are on our way to Middleton. Do you know that town?'

'Aye, it is a longish step though, and on such a night.'

'Weather and miles mean little to me,' John said, and it was a remark one could believe, he was so big. 'Besides, I am used to travel.'

'I have heard that you had seen other places,' said father.

John laughed. 'You will never say a truer word, and all for free. But we go to Middleton to see a man. One like yourself, a weaving fellow. His name is Bamford, Sam Bamford. Will you have heard of him?'

'I have,' said father. 'But he is not a man like me. I hear he is a political fellow and I take no part in that.'

For the first time the other man spoke. 'It takes a part in you, friend, like it or not.'

'Right,' John cried. 'Why, here we sit eating bread and cheese instead of roast beef and carrots, and drinking small beer when it should be good malt ale. Is not that because of politics? Are not laws and prices set for you by rich men? And do you have a say in their making?'

John leaned back triumphantly. Father made no answer and I was surprised. Had he not been saying the same thing to me not half an hour before? I was minded to say as much lest the strangers think us ignorant, but I kept mum in my corner.

'What you say may be true,' father said. 'But you have not walked from Yorkshire to tell me that. Come to your business.'

'It is this—' John leaned forward and placed his hands on his knees. As he did so the sleeves of his coat rucked up and I saw shiny rings on his wrists. At first I thought that they were bangles, and it seemed queer that a man not a gypsy should be wearing them. Then the fire flickered and I saw that they were not bangles but bands of hard skin, like burn scars. John may, I think, have caught my look; at any rate he pulled his hands back quickly and tucked them under his arms.

'Our business,' he said. 'Have you heard of Major Cartwright?'

Father answered that the name did mean something to him but what, exactly, he could not call to mind. At that John told us that the Major was a gentleman in London who had a love for the people and for the liberties of England. He had started a set of clubs where all lovers of freedom could gather together and press the Government to hear them in their just demands. Hampden Clubs they were called, after a great man in the Civil Wars who had stood up for the Parliament against the King of those days.

I was excited at hearing this for it seemed to me a good thing for people to stand together 'loyal and true' as the song goes.

But father gave no sign of pleasure nor displeasure, nor hardly seemed to be listening to John, but stared all the time at the flames of the fire.

At length John ceased telling us of the Major.

'And so,' he said, 'I am going about the country speaking at the clubs and founding new ones where there are none. As we were stepping by, and as I had your name, I thought that we might call on you and ask why the weavers of the moors had no club of their own.'

'Because we have not been so minded, that is all,' answered father. 'Although we may not live like lords up here, yet we do well enough Times are not so bad. I have seen worse.'

Then the other man, he who sat so quietly at the loom, spoke.

'I have seen worse, too. I have seen men hanged for saying that they would not starve. It may not seem so bad now but I think that evil days are coming on us. The French Wars will come to an end and then what will happen?'

Father shrugged. 'Why, peace and prosperity—that is what they say.'

The man laughed. 'Taxes and more taxes are what we will get, friend. The wars have been fought and now they must be paid for—and it is we who will be doing the paying, as we have done the fighting. In the towns we have seen what happens when the rich men get the whip hand over us. You may think that on the moors you will not feel the whip, but you will. You will be beaten down, too, and then have your bones picked bare. Mark my words.'

'Aye. Well, what you say may be true. We will have to wait and see. As to starting a club, when I have thought on it, and if it is not against the law, and if things fall out as you say, well then, I might walk down to Middleton and see this Bamford.'

'No need for that, friend,' said the quiet man. 'I am Bamford.'

I was taken aback by this and stared at the man as gormlessly as a moon-calf. I was astounded that he should have sat so silently while his name was bandied about. Father, though, was unmoved. He looked calmly at Bamford.

'I had a feeling that you might be him. The law has had its hand on you, I believe.'

'That is so,' said Bamford. 'I was taken before the Privy Council of England for daring to speak the truth. I faced Lord Sidmouth and Lord Castlereagh, and the rest of them. I found them no different from other men, and they could find no fault with me. I left them a free man.'

Father mused over this for a moment.

'Well,' he said, 'if things fall out as you say, and I become political, we may meet again. But I have nothing to say now.'

At that the two men rose, and, refusing the offer of a bed—for which I was grateful for it would have been mine—they made off into the night, heeding my father's warning not to call in at the Robin Hood lest there might be dragoons there, who would hold them for the night be their errand never so lawful.

We closed the door on them and on the rain, now driving down, and went back to the fire. I was glad to be there and not with John and Bamford on their long journey down the turnpike into Bury and across the wet fields to Middleton. However, I was not to stay by the fire long for father fished out a coin and bade me go to the Robin Hood and fetch him ale. When I got back he asked me most particularly whether I had seen the two men at the inn, or any other strangers. When I said no, he took his ale and supped some, then leaned back in his chair looking at me. He looked at me for a long time. I knew the look. It was a strange one, as if he was looking through you rather than at you. It was the look he had given me when he set me to work at the mill. It meant that he was thinking mighty carefully of what he had to say, and how he was going to say it. I waited patiently for it did not do to pester him, nor would he ever be hurried. But at length he put down his mug and spoke.

'What you have seen and heard of in here tonight you must not speak of, ever. Do you mind me?'

I wagged my head in answer, being too excited to speak. Father drank more ale and stared at the fire.

'I wish you had not seen those men, nor heard what they had to say. But as you have, I would not like you to think a wrong thing and believe that when I spoke to them of gallow's talk I had in mind robbery or murder. Rather than have you think that I might be a thief, or a murderer, I have it in mind to tell you who that man was, that John, and why it came that I spoke of the gallows. But you must keep your mouth shut. Do you hear?'

I said that I did, although my mouth was open wide enough to drive a waggon into it.

'Well then,' said father. 'You heard me say just now that I had seen worse times than these. So I have, and black times they were. I have seen such times, and I have seen men try to change them. When I was in Spen, before you were born, I joined a brotherhood, one for all. The new machines were coming in and we were hot against them. If a master would not listen to us when we told him not to use the machines, we smashed them. If anyone wished to join us then he swore an oath, "twisting in" we called it, like when you twist many whisps of wool together to get one strong thread. And we called ourselves—'

Here I could not restrain myself for even as I listened I thought of those tales which had haunted my childhood. '—Ludd's men!' I cried.

Father gave me a sharp glance. 'You remember that name, do you? Well, you are not so far from the truth at that. But we called ourselves the Black Lamp, although we would have recognised Ludd had we seen him.'

I leaned forward and took a closer look at my father. Always I had thought him a quiet man, fearless, but no bully, content to think his own thoughts and let others think theirs. But that he should have been in such a brotherhood—I did not know whether I was the more frightened or excited. But then he rose and kicked at the fire which sparked up and threw a red light across his face. He looked a different man then, fierce and formidable, and I could well imagine him marching with a secret army, striking at the tyrants of the machines as Bloom struck at the iron on the anvil.

'I was young in those days,' father went on, 'and I was ready to believe that we could change the world. But the Government sent spies among us; men who ate at our tables and shared our beds and took our oath—and then ran to the magistrates and told all that they had seen.'

His voice shook with anger as he said this and I could share that anger with understanding; for when a poor man shares his bed and his house he shares everything he owns, and the one who would share with him and then betray him is surely worse than a Judas. My father let the bitterness die from his voice and then spoke on as easily as though he was talking of some indifferent topic.

'Some of us they caught. Brother John was one of those. There were others. Lee and Wronkesley got seven years apiece, transported to Australia. Did you see the ring marks on John's wrists? They are where the manacles rubbed his skin. He will wear those rings until the day he dies. And now he has come back. I would never have believed it.'

Again he fell silent and brooded over the fire. The wind had risen and it moaned along the house. The rain it carried tapped on the window. It was as if there was something outside the house, some dark creature of the night wishing to enter. Again I thought of John and Bamford walking the long night miles; perhaps calling at houses here and there with their strange passwords, coming from the night—and the darker past.

As if my father was thinking the same thoughts he suddenly burst out:

'I had thought to have left those things behind me for ever, but see what happens. I have lived quietly for many years and kept my mind from political things. I thought my past was buried deeper than a dead man, and yet it has crawled out and strikes at me again. But it may be as Bamford says. When the Wars end times may be as bad as ever. I do not know. I do not know.'

At that, shaking his head, he rose, and warning me never to speak of these things again he packed me off to bed. The next morning a man, black with mud, galloped through our village with government mails. As he went through he shouted out the news to us. Wellington had beaten the French at Waterloo.

CHAPTER SIX

And so the wars had ended at last. For more than my lifetime armies had marched across Europe and, when they met, had shot each other down like so many lunatics let loose from Bedlam. Kingdoms had been swept away and their kings with them, and peasants had sat on thrones. And now it was all over. Wellington and the Prussian had won and Boney, who had shaken the world with his tread, was lucky to be master of a barren rock.

There were bonfires on the hills that night and the sky was full of golden fire-works. The rich men in Bolton had a great dinner and ate more pies and custards than a regiment could have swallowed. They congratulated themselves on their fortitude during the wars, celebrated the triumph of British arms, sent the Duke of Wellington a golden sword, and threatened the weavers that if they demanded more wages then they would be turned off and left to starve.

In Helmshaw we had no great dinners. A few idlers got drunk, foolish fellows who thought that the French ate babies, but many weavers felt no rejoicing. My father was one of these. He said that Napoleon had given the common man a voice in affairs, and for proof he pointed to the French Marshals; to Ney and Soult, Marmont and Massena.

At first the ending of the wars seemed to have little effect on us in Helmshaw. The wind still blew and the rain fell down on us as though Napoleon had never been. For me it was of more consequence that our old dog Clip died.

I went to the mill as usual. I could take my turn at the forge now and hammer the iron into whatever shape I fancied, and I found out more every day about the mysteries of machinery.

Bloom was a little downcast because the building of the new mill had been postponed for a while. This was because Peel and Fletcher had decided to lay off until they saw what the times of peace would bring.

'They'll come though,' he said, consoling himself. 'Nothing can stop 'em.'

And then, to cheer himself up, he would spend a great deal of his time telling me about the new machines. He told me much about steam-expansion and rotary-motion and pistons and cylinder bores, and all the other things which go to making up the mighty engines. I must confess, though, that I ended with the notion that a fire-engine would be something like a giant kettle, with a spout as big as an elephant's trunk. To turn me into a better engineer Bloom made me learn a great deal of arithmetic. He lent me his sum book and many a night I spent working out its calculations with a piece of chalk on the flagstones in our house.

But although our life seemed unruffled, forces were at work which were to have their effect on us. The spinning mills were turning out thread by the mile, and the clothiers were mad for weavers to turn it into cloth. Everywhere men turned to the loom: farmers let their grazings grow rank, servants ran away from their masters and ostlers from their horses. Men back from the wars turned to weaving and Irishmen settled down to our trade. The towns round about grew and grew and, although we could not see them from our moor, the sky above them was dark with their smoke.

So all seemed well. There was work for everyone, even though it was only weaving fustian, and the days of peace seemed those of plenty, too. But things changed. With so many looms at work the masters began to grow choosy. A week's work might be turned away for some trifling fault and the price paid was less and less. The looms now never cried 'plenty of time', and where a man might once have felt free to stroll out in the air whenever he wished, to have a crack with his neighbour, now he was as securely chained to his machine as any galley-slave to his oar.

Still father missed the worst of this. There were not so many fancy-weavers as to enable the merchants to be too tyrannical and we fared well enough. But then came the taxes. It was as Bamford had said. The wars had been fought, now they were to be paid for. The taxes came upon us like an endless drizzle, so gentle that you do not notice it until you are soaked to the skin. Beer was taxed, bread was taxed, meat was taxed, everything we ate and wore was taxed. Even the windows through which came the light we worked by, even they were taxed. And as the taxes came, so were we all beaten down, and down, and down, until it seemed we would never rise again but stay for ever on our knees. Where once a man, having taken his cloth to the warehouse and sold it, would perhaps have had a drink with the merchant as an equal, now it was caps off when you spoke to them. It was that, I think, which the weavers hated the most. We were used to looking a man in the eyes and damning him if we did not like him. Now we saw ourselves slipping down into common servants, dancing attendance on those, like Cranley, who we hardly regarded as our equals.

Those were bitter days. We lived on a mash of gruel and turnips, like pigs, and ate black bread. Decent men like Sam Teller walked the streets as ragged as sweeps and began staying indoors on Sunday for shame of being seen in their rags. I took to watching father, waiting for him to act on Bamford's words, but he bore it all stubbornly. Then two things happened which I must tell you of.

The first thing is this: I was paid a few coppers a week by Cranley, and Bloom used to give me a few more each Friday. Father had always allowed me to keep these, being content to pay our outgoings from the good money he earned. But one night he came back from Bolton with his pack still on his back. It seemed that the merchants there had turned away all fancy work, saying that they had stocks they could not get rid of. This was a lie for there was a demand for our cloth. Father had then gone into Manchester and had been offered a price so low that it hardly paid for the wool, let alone the weaving. It was plain that the merchants there were hand in glove with the Bolton men to keep down the price and break the fancy-weavers.

Father was bitter that night, saying little and not bothering to set his Jacquard cards for the next day's work. A week's labour and a thirty mile walk for nothing can do that to a man. When it was dark, with Emma in her bed and we preparing for ours, he stood before me with an air such as I had never seen on him before: a hang-dog, nervous manner such as it saddened me to see. As I kicked out the fire he suddenly blurted out that if I had any money he would be needing it. I made nothing of that and gave what I had, but when I was in my bed I felt as bitter as he did. It is not good for a son to see his father humiliated, nor is it good for the father to be so seen.

The second thing is this:

In our village lived an old gaffer called Caleb Whitelaw. He claimed to be a hundred years old, and, whether he was or not (and we had only his word for it) it is certain that he was an ancient. He used to boast that he had marched with Bonnie Prince Charlie when he was down our way and, when he was roaring drunk, that he had been with the Old Pretender in 1715. Like many an old man he was somewhat short of temper, but he took a fancy to an infant named Billy Rowley. Billy, too, was usually none too placid, and it may have been that which made a bond between them. At any rate the two of them used to sit for many an hour in Caleb's garden, usually silent, but sometimes with Caleb roaring down Billy's ear about the daredevil days he had seen with the Jacobites.

It was a funny sight you know, and pleasing, too. Folk used to smile when they saw the two of them together and speculate how Billy would take it when Caleb died. But when, one bleak February, the spotted fever came, in the way that it has, it stepped over the old man and carried the child away.

Well, there was nothing for it but to take Billy down to Haslingden and give him his burial. In a small place, where everyone knows everyone else, no one goes to the grave on his own and so, when we had knocked up a coffin and placed it on a hand-cart, everyone who could lined up to go to the graveyard.

We fell in decently and set off through the village. When we got to Caleb's house Billy's father stopped.

'Old Caleb will wish to say good-bye to the lad,' he said, and went to fetch the old man.

He walked up the path but before he got to the door Caleb tottered out. We were amazed at his dress: for he had on a vast top-coat, blue once but now green with age, on his head he wore a strange hairy bonnet, and he was clutching a battered old sword. Dressed like that he might indeed have been a ghost new-risen from Culloden Moor! Using the sword as a stick he announced that he was coming to Haslingden with us. Everyone tried to dissuade him for it was a long walk, and on such a day, with the air full of a freezing fog, he might well catch his death of cold. But talk as we might he would not listen to us and there was nothing for it but for him to come.

We set off again but before we had gone five hundred yards Caleb's legs failed him and he fell down in the mud. Again we tried to get him to go home but again he refused.

'I am a-coming,' he piped. 'I will get there. I will crawl if need be.' And then he went rambling on about how he had marched to Derby with the Prince and his wild High Landers.

We all looked at him and wondered what to do, for he could not walk, yet we did not wish to leave him—by now it seemed right that he should come if it was at all possible. Then Billy's father solved our problem. He lifted Caleb up and set him on the cart.

'There, Gaffer,' he said. 'You can have a ride down with us.'

He tucked the old man's clothes in and we went on our way. It was a queer sight to see Caleb on the cart with his strange hat, and there were one or two crooked smiles as we went along. As we got down into the valley, we came into heavy mist. We could not see more than fifty yards ahead but we could hear, and it was not long before we heard a sound familiar to us: the jingle of harness.

A minute or two later four dragoons, armed to the teeth with muskets and sabres, loomed out of the mist. They were led by a blue-chinned Irish sergeant. At the sight of us they pulled up. The sergeant, who looked as if there was little left in this world to surprise him, raised his eyebrows at the sight of Caleb. We, for our part, scowled up at him for we hated the dragoons.

'Get off the road,' the sergeant barked in a thick brogue. 'Get you over there.' And he pointed to the ditch.

We looked at him astounded.

'Get in the ditch?' father cried. 'What for?'

'Never you mind. Do as you are ordered and be quick about it,' said the sergeant.

Thomas Spencer, who was another friend of my father, elbowed forward.

'Man,' he cried. 'Can you not see that we are going to a funeral? We have a dead child here,' and he pointed to the coffin.

The sergeant looked into the cart but what he saw made no difference.

'I can't help that,' he growled. 'The Lord Sheriff of the County is coming along here. Now move over or we must move you.'

Thomas went white with rage when he heard that, but Billy's father held his arm.

'Let it be, Thomas,' he said. 'Let the great man come along and we will look at him. It will be an interesting sight for he will be going to hell.'

The sergeant looked sharp then.

'Mind your tongue,' he ordered. 'The Sheriff is the King's representative and you are close to treason.'

He stood over us while we pulled into the ditch and then rode on. A little later a dozen cavalry came past, and then a coach pulled by four horses, with a group of the Yeomanry by it. The horses were having a hard time of it on the steep hill. The coachman was cursing and laying his whip across them but as the coach drew level with us it ground to a halt in the heavy mud. The blinds on the weather side of the coach were down, but on our side they were up and we could see the interior.

It was a strange sight to see on that bleak day. Inside, the coach glowed with colour like a cock's neck. It was padded with red sateen and lolling back against this were four gentlemen dressed in red and blue and green. Their neckcloths were as white as snow and they wore periwigs sparkling with powder. Underneath these their faces shone with good living. They had crystal glasses in their hands and were drinking some rich purple drink. To me it was a sight as strange as Ali Baba's cave and I stared in wonder, half dazed by its splendour. One of the men caught sight of us and made a gesture as if to wave us away, but then saw Caleb perched on the cart. He craned forward and tittered. The others looked up at that, and they too peered at us, crowing with laughter.

My father raised his fists to his forehead in a kind of agony. He raised his fists then seized the coffin and held it up to view.

'Laugh at this,' he shouted.

Immediately a look of disgust crossed the faces of the gentlemen. They turned away and one of them stretched out a white hand and pulled down the blind.

As if that were a signal, the horses gave a huge heave and pulled the coach free and away up the hill. We stared after it with, I swear, murder in our hearts. Then Caleb roused himself. He lurched forward and threw his sword at the coach. It was a feeble throw. Indeed the sword hardly cleared the side of the cart and it fell harmlessly to the road. But behind the coach were more soldiers and one of them saw the sword fall.

On the instant he had his sabre clear and had pulled his horse over to us.

'Hold still,' he bellowed. 'Or you are dead men!'

The men burst into bitter laughter at that and indeed it was ridiculous enough, seeing the dragoon in his great overcoat rearing over us on his horse, waving his sabre in the air, and threatening a handful of half-starved weavers and one crazy old man. It became even more ridiculous when Caleb began a long harangue about the iniquities of Butcher Cumberland. The dragoon looked around, bewildered, only to meet amused smiles from his comrades. An officer came over and asked what was going on.

'They attacked the coach,' said the dragoon, but with no conviction in his voice.

My father laughed at that. 'It was the old man,' he said. 'He dropped his sword. See.' He stepped forward and picked up the weapon. 'He is an old soldier, and a little crazy.'

The officer looked down at us thoughtfully.

'What have you in there?' he asked, meaning the coffin.

'My son,' said Billy's mother. 'Maybe you would like to see him.'

The officer turned his head away when he heard that.

'Move off,' he said in a thick voice. 'But keep your weapons at home the next time you go to a funeral.'

Somewhat shamefacedly he fumbled in his pocket and threw a coin down at us. My father looked at it deliberately, then ground it into the mud with his heel. He stared then at the officer. He, though, would not meet the gaze and turned away, calling the men after him.

We went down to Haslingden, buried Billy and then trudged home. The rest of the village gathered in Billy's house but my father walked on, like a sleep-walker, down to Middleton. There he spoke to Bamford, and when he came home he founded a Hampden Club in our village.

CHAPTER SEVEN

In truth we had been pinched and starved but it was not this alone that led my father down to Middleton. Before, we had borne hardship and, no doubt, we would have suffered it again in silence; but the events of Billy's funeral marked father and drove him into the political way. It was a blow not at his belly, but at his humanity and, I believe, he founded the Club to defend not his purse, but his dignity.

I believe this is so for I think nothing else would have led him to become prominent in Clubs. He was, do you see, a man with a past better hidden and to lead men in politics was a sure way of coming to the notice of the authorities—and who knew what would happen then?

Be that as it may, the Club cost a penny a week to join. Every club was in a union of its District so no one club felt alone. The money we paid was pooled to buy a paper, the *Political Register*, which was written by William Cobbett. This became our Bible. Every word Cobbett wrote seemed to strike at the very heart of our troubles for he spoke of the liberties of the people and of the weapon that the people had to fight for them—the Reform of Parliament.

We Radicals, for such we were called, had weekly meetings to read the paper and discuss it. I read it as eagerly as any weaver for I was as little pleased as they when I breakfasted on gruel and black bread and came home to a plate of turnips instead of meat and wheaten bread. I was still less pleased when I discovered that I could not have a new coat but must make do with my old one, which was patched all over.

Cranley, of course, knew that we had a club, for we made it

no secret, and he used to mention it in a dirty, jeering, sort of way.

'So thou hast a Parliament up i' the Tops, now,' he would cry. 'Who be Prime Minister, then? Tha father?'

I turned a deaf ear to this talk. I thought it the scorn of one weaker than I, and the reason I thought that was because the Reform Clubs were becoming stronger every day. My father was not alone in feeling that humiliation of the spirit, such as he endured on the day of Billy's burial. Others, who felt the same deep injuries, were also turning to politics, in defence of their manhood as much as of their pockets.

One day I was at my work-bench when I heard the clatter of horses. Looking through the window I saw Colonel Fletcher, the Magistrate of Bolton, ride into the yard. I glowered through the glass for I thought him one of our enemies, then turned back to my work. Within a minute I heard my name called. I went out and found Fletcher talking to Cranley.

'Here, you,' Cranley called, giving a detestable jerk of the head.

I went over and stood sullenly before them. It is hard to say how discontented I felt standing there. Fletcher towered above me on his glossy horse, dressed in fine worsted and snow-white linen, while I, ragged and unkempt, dirty from my work, dressed in fustian, stood like a slave at the level of his boots. There is something about a man on horseback that is truly hateful. He sits above like a king on a throne, looking down on lesser mortals. In truth I was sick of seeing men, soldiers and landlords and mill-owners, prance about our valley as if it belonged to them.

Cranley gave me a push.

'Show some respect,' he cried.

How I was to do this was not clear to me. I had no hat to doff and short of dropping on my knees I could not think what to do. At any rate I lowered my gaze since it seemed that simply looking at the gentry was now a crime, like looking at the Emperor of China.

Fletcher stared at me then waved his whip.

'Turn round,' Cranley barked.

I slowly shuffled around, my face red with temper. Fletcher said nothing but pulled his horse away, dismounted, and went into the counting-house. I turned to Cranley and asked him why Fletcher had wished to look at me.

'Why,' he said, 'The Colonel is going shares in the new mill. You will be working on his machines and he wishes to see what sort of creature he will be hiring. If you were buying a dog to mind those tups your father has on the moor you'd want to see it first, wouldn't you?'

With that he slouched after Fletcher. I went back to my bench and got to work with my file. The reference to a dog I took without too much rancour. It was the sort of language a real dog like Cranley used naturally. Indeed it was a sort of compliment. At least I had been compared to a living thing. Most men in Cranley's eyes were no more than sticks or stones, their only value lying in how much money could be wrung from them. The real offence, for me, was in being forced to wait upon another's whim, to have to come and go as he pleased. I jabbed sullenly at a piece of iron and lost myself in my work until I found Bloom tapping me on the shoulder.

'There's summat wrong in the spinning-room,' he said. 'Come and see if you can spot it.'

I followed him and we stood among the din of the machines. Bloom stretched out his arms and pointed. His lips moved and, although the noise was so great, I knew he was saying, 'Over there'. Reading lips that is called and everyone in the mills knows how to do it for speech there is impossible, the noise being so great.

I cocked my head and listened intently, for an engineer learns as much through his ears as his eyes. As much as any living creature a machine has its own voice. It clatters and roars and tinkles, but, always, it has a rhythm unlike any other machine —and if that rhythm alters then there is something wrong with the machine.

After a while I thought I heard something wrong, a discordant note in one of the water-frames. I turned to tell Bloom but he had slipped away across the room. As I lifted my head, though, I caught sight of Burns, the overseer of the children. He had hold of a child and was thrashing her with his stick. It was a sight which I had seen often enough before. Beatings and hunger and exhaustion, brutality, all these were part of the mill, growing from it as naturally as leaves from a tree. But I was growing up. I was learning that some, at least, of the cruelties of the world were not a part of nature but were created to line the pockets of villains like Cranley, and to buy fine chargers for such as Fletcher. For the first time I felt that the children were, in some sort, my responsibility and seeing one so cruelly ill-treated made me flush with anger. I wished to strike a blow at the mill, at Burns, and at his masters.

Every engineer carries scraps of metal in his pockets. Hardly thinking, I fished a piece out and threw it into the heart of the machinery. Straightaway there was a terrible screeching, scraping noise. The machine ground to a halt, its spindles and bobbins flew off, the driving-belt snapped with a harsh crack, and the yarn flew all over the place.

Even above this din I heard the children screaming. They ran back from the machines and cowered against the wall. Burns stared at the wreckage pop-eyed, his stick idle. I, too, was taken aback. For a moment I gaped at the chaos and then did that which contradicted what I had done. I ran into the wheel house and threw off the gears which connected the mules to the water-wheel.

At once the grinding of the machines stopped. I could still hear the children crying, men calling, the roar of the brook in the mill-race, but louder than anything I heard my own breath for I was panting as hard as though I had wrestled with Jacob's angel. I was frightened, too, by what I had done, but I calmed myself and, putting on a bold face, went back into the spinning-room.

Bloom was there and Cranley was with him. Cranley was staring madly at the tangled mess.

'What happened?' he bawled, his voice thick with rage.

Bloom shook his head. 'I don't know. I thought that there was something wrong. We were just listening for it.' He turned to me. 'Did you hear it, Daniel?'

'Yes,' I answered. 'I heard a machine sound wrong, I heard it plain, and then it went.'

This statement did nothing to calm Cranley.

'Look!' he bellowed. 'Look!' He shook his fist at the frames and, indeed, they were a sorry sight. Thread and yarn lay over them like gossamer.

Bloom spread his arms out wide.

'No use shouting, Master Cranley,' he said calmly. 'Machines do break and that is all there is to it. We must just set to and mend them.'

He looked thoughtfully at the frames and I could hardly stop a smile at his expression, it was such a mixture of anguish at the mess, and joy at the prospect of a good engineering task.

'You threw the gears, did you?' he asked me.

I answered, 'Yes,' and he gave me a slap on the shoulder.

'There now,' he said. 'It is as well we have a lad with a good head on his shoulders or it could all be worse. And now we must set to and mend things.'

And that was that. Cranley might have a face as black as thunder but there was nothing he could do except storm from the room. Then Bloom and I set to our work. We called in some children to clear away the cotton and plunged into the heart of the machinery. It did not take Bloom long to find the cause of the trouble.

'See here,' he said. 'This gear is all bunged up.'

He scraped out a twist of metal and looked at it carefully.

'Now where did that come from?'

I was anxious that Bloom should not be too inquisitive.

'Why,' I said, as casually as I could, 'it is a scrap of metal from the machine. It must have got shaved off when the machine jammed.'

Bloom pulled his face. 'I doubt that. This is lead and there is no lead in that frame.'

I felt my heart sink as he said this.

'Oh, then it must have got there by mistake.'

'A funny mistake,' Bloom answered. 'I'll tell you what I think, Daniel: I think someone threw this lead into the machine for to break it.' He looked at me through his slaty eyes. 'It was deliberate, and that is a hanging matter.'

'Why,' I said, and my voice was dry and chokey. 'Who here would do that?'

'Who is to say?' said Bloom. 'Anyone of these children could have done it. Maybe one of them has the sense to know that they cannot work when the machines do not.'

'Will you be telling Cranley?' I asked, and my voice trembled with fear.

Bloom gave me a long steady look.

'Maybe this lead did get in the frame by mistake, as you think. Maybe it is not lead at all. No need to bother the master with it.'

I heaved a sigh of relief at that, you may be sure, but Bloom had not finished with me.

'If someone had thrown lead into the machine and it could be proved, that would be like Luddism—and the Luddites went to the rope. Next time someone might do so.'

For a time after that we worked on in silence. It took the best part of the day to sort things out but, at length, we were finished. We made a new part for the frame, remounted the spindles, and jointed the driving-belt. Bloom hung over the frame, intent as a heron over a pool. Finally he nodded, stepped back, and ran his eye speculatively along the shaft which carried the driving-belt to each individual machine.

'It looks all right,' he said, 'but we had best check the shafts before we start the machines going. They might have had a shaking. You get on with that, and see that you look at them all. You never know what might have happened. Go through the whole mill. I don't want any more barneys with the master.'

With that he stalked off, leaving me to get on with it. I got an old box to stand on and began working my way through the mill. Each floor had its own shaft, connected to the main shaft which ran from the big gears to the water-wheel. The top floor of our mill had a row of Arkwright's water frames and two or three of Crompton's mules which Cranley was trying out. Everything seemed in order there and so I went down to the ground floor where we had the heavy machines. There was the carding machine which combed out the raw wool after it had been washed, and the felting hammers, huge wooden mauls in tubs, which beat the loose woven cloth into a smooth matted fabric.

I looked carefully at every joint in the shaft and satisfied myself that they were secure. Beyond the felting hammers there was a long narrow passage, open on one side, where we had a double row of tenter frames. These were wooden beams bristling with thousands of fine nails, tenterhooks as they are called, on which the finished cloth was spread to be stretched into the final lengths. At the end of the passage was another room where we kept the carding machine. We had rigged up a shaft down the tenter frames to this machine and, although it hardly seemed likely that this shaft could have been damaged, I minded Bloom's injunction and took myself down there to look at it.

I took my box and ducked under the cloth which hung on the frames and looked at first one joint, then another. I had to go carefully for it would have been easy to get caught on the nails. Many a time I had seen the children do it as they wrestled with the heavy cloth-lengths, and get a row of holes in their hands for their pains.

I had neared the end of the shaft and was about to jump down from my box when I heard the clash of clogs on the flag-stones. At first I thought that it was Bloom and I was about to call him, but I caught the softer tread of leather boots and hesitated. Just by me, on the other side of the cloth, the footsteps stopped, and I saw the cloth jerk.

'What are you looking for?' asked Fletcher's voice.

In answer there came Cranley's coarse growl: 'Faults.'

'Do you find many?'

'You can always find something if you look hard enough.'

'And if you want to.'

'Aye,' Cranley said. 'Then you can knock something off the wages for a fine.'

Fletcher laughed, a soft genteel titter. 'And where there are none, you can always . . . provide them.'

'Aye, but I don't tell the weavers that.' Cranley laughed too, a dirty sort of guffaw, but no worse than Fletcher's cultivated squeak.

'You look as if you might find many today, Cranley. This mess has not sweetened you.'

'Damn me, that it hasn't. For two pins I would turn Bloom off.'

'Come now,' said the Colonel. 'He is a good engineer, you have told me so yourself. We will need him for the new engines, remember. Besides he has made a good job of this, today.'

'Maybe,' Cranley's answer was surly. 'But machines do not just break down for nothing. He has not been attending to his work. I shall fine him for this. I shall dock him a week's wages. Damn it, I have lost seventy pounds by this.'

'I would not be so quick,' answered Fletcher, 'or he might take himself off. Good millwrights do not grow on trees you know. Keep him until we find another, anyway.'

Cranley muttered something which I did not catch. They moved around for a moment and then Cranley spoke again.

'Well, you have seen that young whelp, Cregg.'

When he said that I thought, for a moment, that they had seen me behind the cloth, and I almost blurted out that I was working. But Fletcher answered:

'Yes, a surly young brute like all these moorland creatures. A touch of the whip would do him no harm.'

'He needs more than a touch. But he keeps his mouth as tight shut as a bull-dog. I have questioned him about his father but he lets nothing slip.'

'Be patient, man. No doubt his father has told him to keep his mouth shut—if his father is who you say he is.'

Cranley grunted. 'I tell you I know him. I saw him in Yorkshire with the Black Lamp.'

47

'At night, by torch-light, and nineteen years ago.'

'I would swear to it,' Cranley growled.

'Would you?' Fletcher sounded sceptical. 'I should think again about that. Juries are not so easy to persuade now as they were when they saw a Jacobin under every bed. If they let Cregg go free, you might end up in the dock yourself, charged with perjury.'

'If his father was not a Luddite as I say then where did the lad get his notions? He threatened me with Ludd's name and now, damn me, he is in my mill and it has been smashed. I have a mind to get the lad and thrash the truth from him.'

'Now keep your head,' said Fletcher sharply. 'Would they be foolish enough to play Ludd here? In a mill under our very noses? No. Anyway, it is all this Hampden Club nonsense now. Keep calm, man. Cregg is sticking his nose out with this political business and we may get him there, or we may hear something from Yorkshire which will support your word.'

'You seem not too interested in this affair.' Cranley's voice was full of sour antagonism. 'Remember, when the new mill is built, your money will be at stake.'

'Don't be foolish.' Fletcher was sharp. 'There is nothing I would like more than to put my hands on the rascal. All these village politicians are a nuisance but this man is dangerous. He knows what he is about and such men are a menace to the whole country. But I have no wish to appear a fool. Oil the lad, butter him up, and he will let something slip. And then we will have the pair of them.'

I stood on my box, absorbed in what I had heard. So Cranley knew of my father and the Black Lamp. And I had been given my job so that I might be pumped and my father hanged!

And then Cranley gave a vicious curse and in a rage he wacked at the cloth with his stick. The noise startled me and, without thinking, I swayed back from it. I felt the box teeter under me and I grabbed at the frame. Even then I was cool enough not to put my hands on the nails but grabbed the frame underneath. But I was carried too far and my face landed full on the nails.

A bubbling cry of pain rose in my throat but I suffocated it. Nothing seemed more important to me than that I should not be discovered, that I should be able to tell my father what I had heard without Cranley or Fletcher knowing. I felt sick with pain, but I held on—and on—until I heard Cranley's clogs crash away down the corridor. My mouth sticky with blood, I plucked my cheek away from the nails and fell onto the floor, squatted for a few moments, and then rose. My face throbbed and burned. I put my hand on my cheek. When I pulled it away, I saw that the blobs of blood formed a red dotted line. I could not show myself with that badge on my cheek, one glance would show where the wound had been gained. Trying not to think, I ran down the passage into the carding room, found a scrap of metal, and scraped it across the nail holes. It hurt less than I had thought. The pain seemed to be inside, pulsing away there, but hidden, secret.

I wandered back down the passage and into the workshop. Bloom was there. He cocked an eye at my bloody cheek and examined it passionlessly, as if it were a damaged machine. Without a word he took my arm and led me to the trough where we kept clean water and ducked my head in it. He peered at it again and turned to Cranley and Fletcher who were talking to each other by the counting house.

'The lad has had a nasty knock,' he cried.

Cranley slouched over and stared at my cheek.

'Why, that's nothing,' he growled. ''Tis nought but a scratch.'

'It's more than a scratch,' Bloom answered. 'He needs to rest himself. Will you let him be off?'

Cranley opened his mouth wide at that. 'Off?' he shouted. 'Off where?'

'Off home.' Bloom said.

'Home!' cried Cranley, as flabbergasted as if Bloom had said 'Heaven'. He fished out his watch.

'Why, 'tis not yet turned four. Am I to give half a day off to every rascal that can't look where he is going. Turn to and get to your work. I have lost a hundred pounds already today.'

I was ready enough to go back to my work, for I would not have asked Cranley for the leaving of his dog's dinner were I starving, but Bloom was firm.

'Come now, Master,' he said. 'If it were not for the boy being quick-thinking, we might have no mill left to work in.'

'Aye,' roared Cranley, his temper rising. 'And whose fault is that, hey? Who do I pay two pounds a week to look after the machines? Tell me that.'

Bloom was quite undaunted by this.

'If you would stop the machines sometimes, then I might have time to go over them. But if you do not like my work, why then, I will be off.'

There was all the makings of a good row but Fletcher strolled across.

'Now then, Cranley,' he said. 'Let the lad have the day off. He has done you a good turn this day.' And he gave Cranley a sly nudge in the ribs.

Cranley turned sharply, ready to fire his guns at Fletcher, too, but when he saw the look on Fletcher's face, such a sly, smooth look, he halted.

'Aye,' he said, 'aye, maybe you're right. I spoke a bit hasty like.'

He turned to me with a disgusting sort of smile on his face.

'Go off Daniel, lad. Have a lie down. Put some vinegar on that cut and you'll be right as rain.' And the villain slapped me on the back as if I was the best friend he had in the world.

'That's right,' said Fletcher. 'And have tomorrow morning off as well if you don't feel right.'

Cranley's face went green at that but he choked back his feelings as well as he could and nodded assent. I went to the bench room for my coat, feeling that I had done well out of the day's events. I put my coat on and went back across the yard. The three men were standing by the carding room where the mules were roaring away like thunder.

'It sounds all right now,' Bloom was saying.

'Yes,' Fletcher answered. 'It makes a good roar. It beats me how you men manage to talk to each other in there. Mister Cranley and I were talking when the machines started up and the row drove us clean out. We couldn't hear a blessed word we were saying!'

CHAPTER EIGHT

I ran home at a jog-trot, for I was desperately anxious to tell my father what I had heard. When I was by our house, though, I paused for there were two men lounging by the front door. I crossed over, ready to keep on walking if they were to turn out to be spies, but when I got close I recognised one of them. He was a small man with a sharp face, half hidden under a mangy hat. It was Healey, a friend of Bamford's. He called himself a doctor and surgeon but I would sooner have trusted him to dress my hair than any wound, for all the doctoring he knew was a few simples. The other fellow I did not know. He was a hulking man who looked stronger in the arm than the head.

Seeing Healey, I was not surprised when I got in our house to find Bamford himself there, nor to see the house full of men from our village. I was curious when I saw Obadiah Briggs squatting in a corner. All the others present were in the Club, but Briggs and his flock had steered clear so far. Seeing Briggs, though, gave me a shock. None of us in the room looked well fed or well clothed, but Briggs had on his face a true mask of starvation. Although I did not like the man, nor his canting ways, I felt a pang of pity seeing him like that and it made me reflect on how those men got on who were in the common line of weaving.

I slipped through the men and went to my father. I tugged at his elbow but he shrugged me off and would not be bothered with me at that time. Thoughtlessly I accepted this and left him to go into the scullery and cut myself a piece of cheese. Then I stood in the doorway, munching and listening to what was going on.

Bamford had risen and was standing on a stool, telling the men about a great meeting which was to be held in Manchester.

'All Reform men will be there,' he said. 'There will be folk from Bolton and Preston, Oldham, Ashton, Middleton, men from Yorkshire and all over the North. We mean to demand the right to have a say over our own affairs and to show the Government that we will not be treated as slaves.'

Our men growled their approval at that—as who would not? —but when Bamford reminded us again that we were being taxed to death to pay for the French Wars, Obadiah Briggs stood up.

'I come here as delegate from the Saints of Heytop,' he said in his whining voice. 'I speak for them all and I say nay, nay, to what you have said. 'Tis not we who pay all these taxes. I pay none at all, nor do any of the Saints, not one penny between us. 'Tis the rich men like Cranley that does pay the taxes.'

Bamford went quite red when he heard this.

'Why, man,' he shouted in an exasperated way. 'Do you not eat? Do you not use candles and coals? And are they not taxed? Or do the ravens bring them for you as they brought bread for Elijah?'

'The ravens bring us nought,' said Briggs, 'as you well know. 'Tis true we pay taxes on our stuff, but so too does Master Cranley, and, since he eats more than we do and burns more coals, 'tis right and proper that he should have the say over us.'

With that he looked around triumphantly, with the air of one who has given an invincible blow.

Some of our men looked uneasy when they heard Briggs' speech, for it had a ring of truth about it. Bamford though was equal to it.

'Man,' he cried. 'In this village you eat more food in a week than Cranley could in a six-month, though he were to stuff himself like ten pigs. Do you not see that? And the taxes, to Cranley they are nothing, but to you they are a half of what you earn.'

A mutter went around the room at that. Indeed it was true and there was no gainsaying it. Even Briggs knew it and so he sank to his haunches, having nothing more to say.

Bamford then looked around in a challenging sort of way, as if to say that anyone who wished might put a question and be dealt with as Briggs had been. He was not disappointed of his wish for James Adshead rose to his feet.

'Are you saying that we shall rule the land?' he asked. 'I doubt that we could do that. 'Tis the lords and the gentry that do the ruling; they are bred for it. I could not rule the land.'

'Well,' Bamford said, 'as to that, I can say that there are many who are neither lords nor gentry who have more sense in them than many a baron. But who are these lordlings? In Saxon times there were none. All were equal and had their say and the land was well ruled. And take America! Do they have lords there? None that I have ever heard of but are they badly led? They beat a dozen British lords in the Independence War and captured our commander, Lord Cornwallis himself, and all his army, and the man that beat him was nought but a farmer who had left his plough for a season. But there every man has a vote and so he learns the use of it. 'Tis like the weaving, I think. A boy cannot learn the loom by looking at it. He has to throw the shuttle himself. It may be that he will make mistakes at first but he will end up a weaver as the Americans have ended up statesmen.'

'Have you been to America, then?' asked Thomas Spencer, who was always one for an awkward question.

'That I have not,' said Bamford, squarely enough. 'But many men have, and lived well. And Cobbett was there.'

At Cobbett's name everyone fell silent; there was no denying him. After a moment Bamford spoke up again.

'You have heard what I have had to say. Will you come to the meeting, or will the men of the moors be left behind?'

The men were silent at that. To sit in Helmshaw talking of high taxes and low wages was one thing. To march down to Manchester and demand the vote was quite another. Yet there was no gainsaying the truth of what Bamford had said. Finally a man asked whether Cobbett would be at the meeting.

'No,' said Bamford, 'I think not. But Hunt, the great orator, will be there, and Mr. Carlisle, the writer, and many another gentleman.'

Then my father, who had said nothing until then, stood up.

'Is this meeting in the law?' he asked.

'Why, yes it is.' said Bamford.

My father looked around the little room. His eyes travelled

from one gaunt face to another, from one ragged body to the next. For a moment he looked at me. He moved his arms out a little and turned his palms upwards in a gesture half resigned, half beseeching.

'Well then,' he said. 'I for one will go.'

For the moment there was a profound stillness in the room, a sense, as it were, of something happening so important that none could comprehend it, although all might be aware of it. Then Kenneth Adshead raised his hand, and Thomas Spencer, and Henry Rowley, and, one by one, all others until the only man in the room with his hand down was Briggs.

'And what of you, friend?' Bamford asked.

Briggs raised his head from between hunched shoulders.

'I cannot say. I must ask the Saints of Heytop and then we will pray for guidance. If it so be that the Holy Spirit does guide us then it may be that we will come.'

Bamford gazed at Briggs quizzically but said no more to him. Instead he addressed himself to the other men.

'To those who will come I should say this. You must elect yourselves a captain———' but before he could finish my father leapt to his feet.

'I want no talk of captains,' he cried. 'No talk of armies.'

'I was not talking of armies,' said Bamford. 'But when we go to Manchester, we must go in order. Those who are against us say that we are a rabble and not worthy of a vote. This march will show that we are decent and orderly, and as responsible as any gentleman. There will be no weapons and no man will be allowed to march under our banners who is drunk. When I talk of a captain I mean only that we shall have a man in each body who will keep order. One who will be listened to. Does anyone here disagree with that?'

No one did. All agreed with Bamford's words and showed it through a babble of talk. Bamford called for silence. He took from his pocket a paper and, asking all present to stand, he read aloud a poem. 'The Lancashire Hymn' he called it. I remember it began:

>   Great God, who did of old inspire
>   The patriot's ardent heart,
>   And filled him with a warm desire

To die, or do his part;
Oh! let our shouts be heard by thee,
Genius of liberty!

Bamford confessed that he had penned these lines himself. For their literary quality I cannot answer but the sentiment was shared by all present except, perhaps, Briggs. To a round of applause Bamford left us, taking with him Healey (who offered to remove bad teeth from any Reformer at a low price) and the other man, who was some form of bodyguard.

When the three of them had gone, my father was unanimously elected captain of the Helmshaw Reformers and the men marched off in a body to the Robin Hood, to celebrate the day's events.

I sat up with Emma until father returned, for I was mad to tell him of what I had heard at the mill. It was late when he got back and then he brought one or two friends. Seeing me still up he told me to go to bed, and so there was nothing for it but to mount the stairs. For a long time I lay awake, listening to the drone of the conversation, but at last hearty voices cried farewell, the door slammed, and father came up.

When I saw the candle glow at the bedroom door I called to him. He came in somewhat impatiently.

'Why are you not asleep?' he asked.

I was so excited I could hardly get the words from my mouth, but I told him of what had happened. When I had finished he stared at me with a face as hard as iron.

'You are sure of this? Sure?' he said.

I nodded and then my father did that which I had not heard him do more than half a dozen times in my life—he swore.

'Damn me,' he cried. Damn me! Why did you not tell me this when you got home?'

His voice was so hard and frightening that I could scarce stammer out my excuse:

'I did want to tell you but you shrugged me off, and then you went out.'

At that he sat down on the edge of the bed and his face softened somewhat.

'Well, maybe that is so. You should have told me but it is no use expecting old heads on young shoulders. If I had known

55

then what you have heard, though, I doubt that I would have been so quick to say I would go on this march, and I would not have agreed to be captain. It is a little like putting my head on the block.'

'You can say that you have changed your mind,' I suggested.

He shook his head firmly.

'No, that would never do. I have given my word and to break it would be like breaking my heart. I must do as I have promised.'

For a while he brooded, running his hand across his chin. 'I do not think there can be so much danger in this. If there had been real evidence, then I would have been on the scaffold long since. I wonder, though, what part Cranley plays in this. You say he believed that he had seen me?'

I nodded assent to this.

'It is a strange thing, then. To think that all these years Cranley has been walking about these parts holding that secret to his breast. I wonder what part he played in those days? It may be that there is that in his own past which will not bear looking at too closely. I might make my own enquiries about him, for two can play at that game. As for you, you must go to your work as usual, but you must guard your tongue. Say nothing, do you mind me?'

I assured him that I did.

'And you will go on the march?' I asked.

'Aye, I shall go,' he answered grimly. 'A man may as well be hanged as clem to death.' And with that he went to bed.

CHAPTER NINE

The next day I went to work somewhat nervously, but when Cranley saw me, he merely grunted and told me to make up for lost time. I was more than ready to do that because it kept me out of his way. For that day, and for many another, I worked hard, always on edge, waiting for Cranley to start pumping me or for Fletcher to ride up and arrest me on a warrant. And every night when I went home it was with fear lest father should have been taken. But nothing happened and my fears were forgotten in two great excitements.

One of these was the preparations for the fire-engines. The new mill was almost complete and men from Watt and B. had come up to make sure that everything was perfect. The coming of the machines filled Bloom's horizon but they occupied only a corner of mine, for the centre of my life was the great March.

There was much to be done in preparation for our demonstration, much to-ing and fro-ing. Delegates from other villages in our Union were forever meeting with us and men from all parts of Lancashire and Yorkshire, and as far away as Carlisle, took to calling in and spending the night. Bamford called often, for as leader of the weavers he bore the heavy responsibility and was determined to see that all was done within the law. Among our callers was Brother John and, in his wake, came others whose presence made me uneasy.

Why this should be so is not easy to say. The men were like any others: they dressed in fustian and clogs, ate what there was, slept on the floor, and spoke decently of Reform—but still, I did not like them. They were men without jobs or trades, homes or families, and I have never liked such men. Nor did I like it when

I saw them with father, sitting in corners, whispering, and looking always over their shoulders as if in fear of being overheard.

But despite these forebodings the world seemed a better, more hopeful place for the March. News of it had even reached the pauper children of the mill, and they looked up and seemed sprightlier, for I do believe that they thought all the men in the world were going to march on the Government and demand their freedom and they would for ever after live on plum pudding, treacle, and bacon.

I say that not to scorn the mites for if they were ignorant—and how could they not be?—then there were men in our village who were hardly less so. Indeed there were grown men who thought that all the lords of the government would be in Manchester dressed in coronets and ermine; and that when they saw the steady ranks of the marchers, they would throw away their wands of office and give all to us. But such men were few. Most of the moor weavers were steady fellows, and if some did not know all they might about why they were marching, they joined in at least out of trust in those men they knew—men such as Bamford and my father.

We had got to hear that all the towns in the Unions were to march under their own banners and we determined to do the same. My father, himself, wove a bolt of cloth as smooth as damask and the women set to embroidering it. Thomas Spencer, who was a fair hand with a pencil, designed our symbol. This was of two hands clasped together in loving friendship over figures of a weaver and a fair woman, she holding a child and a distaff in her hands; this showing the harmony of our families. Above were the words 'Universal Suffrage', which meant a vote for everyone, and, beneath, in large red letters, 'Liberty'. The whole was surrounded by true-love knots in green and white. And every living soul in our village put a thread in the banner. We were well satisfied that whatever other towns might produce in the way of an ensign we need feel no inferiority before them, small though our village might be.

While the women plied the needle, the men spent their leisure hours on the moor, drilling under the command of Sam Teller, who had been a corporal in the 82nd Foot, for we wished to be able to go in proper order when we went on our great adventure. Sam drilled us well. We learned to march in file, both at the quick and the slow, turn to the half and the quarter at the word of command, and stand in the rank as steadily as the King's Guards. I do believe that if we had been given more time we could have learned to form the Hollow Square and stand off a charge of cavalry.

One evening when we were drilling we saw four men on horseback canter up. They stood off from us at a distance of a quarter-mile and watched us intently. They were due west from us and with the setting sun behind them it was impossible to make out who they were. They were a disturbing sight, black shapes against the dull red sky, and as sinister as the Four Horsemen of the Apocalypse. We all felt this evil quality for, after at first laughing and jeering, and clapping hands to simulate the shooting of muskets, our men fell silent and stood about uneasily.

James Adshead glared angrily at the riders. 'Come on,' he cried, and led the way across the moor at the watchers. We all followed him, but as we advanced, they trotted off a little distance, and when we moved forward again retreated once more. The men muttered angrily but were baulked. However, an idea entered my head. Without saying a word I slipped away up a fold of the moor. A stream entered this and led to a wall being built by a farmer who was enclosing part of the moor. In turn, this led to another brook. I went down this, keeping my head low, and came to a few straggly rowan trees. I wormed through them and got a clear view of the men. One of them was Colonel Fletcher, dressed in his uniform. With him he had another man from the Yeomanry. A little apart was Cranley, and there was a fourth man, a small wiry fellow with a crooked nose. He had a spy-glass and was busy observing our men. I could not hear what was being said but the man with the crooked nose was gesticulating and the Yeoman with Fletcher was busy scribbling in a book. I took a long look at the little man, impressing his face on my memory, then cut back the way I had come.

When I told them what I had seen, there was a growl of anger. We had been spied on before and it was no surprise that Fletcher, a magistrate, should come sniffing over the moors; but that Cranley should be peeping at us seemed, somehow, a mark of black treachery, he living near us. The third man was, obviously, one of Fletcher's lackeys, but when I mentioned the man with the crooked nose there was a puzzled silence.

'Who might that be?' someone asked.

No one answered but all looked uneasy. Fletcher and Cranley we might hate and see as our enemies; but we knew them, and knowing a thing robs it of half its fearfulness. But this other man brought with him an air of menace, a sense of things bigger than those we knew of, a sign of a world beyond ours which made our small village and its doings of no consequence, made it seem feeble and ineffectual.

'Shall we not leave off our drilling?' asked Sam Teller.

'No,' said father. 'We are breaking no laws by standing on our own commons. As for drilling, they already know we are doing that. But let us be on our guard against strangers for there is no telling who we might be talking to.'

With that we re-formed our ranks and marched steadily across the moor towards the watchers, who turned away at last and cantered off towards Bolton.

That night I played with Emma for a while. I had made her some dolls from iron scraps and it amused her to line them up and make believe that they were the weavers going on the March. She had made, in a childish way, a banner for the toys and we waved it proudly as we moved the dolls to a few old loom-blocks we had built up to represent Manchester. At length father told Emma to go to her bed. With a last 'Huzza!' we scattered the blocks and carried the banner in triumph up the stairs. I read to her for a while from *Gulliver's Travels*, which always delighted her, and when she was soundly sleeping, snuffed out the candle and went downstairs. I sat with father beside the fire. All night he had been quiet, his face clouded and dark. I waited patiently, for I knew he wished to speak, and, by and by, he did.

'That man, the one you saw on the moors: I have it in mind that I know him. If he is who I believe him to be then he is a dog who deserves drowning. When I was in Spen, in those days I told you of, he was one of those who came among us, ready to lead us into desperate adventures—and then to swear our lives away. His name is Castle, and he is a spy!'

When he said this father's face flushed with anger and his voice grew bitter. I saw again the man I had pictured leading the Black Lamp men down from the moors. But it seemed to me then that I saw him not with a musket or a pike, but with a burning sword, like that which guards the Tree of Life in the Garden of Eden.

'I see now,' my father went on, 'what Fletcher meant by saying that there might be someone from Yorkshire who could bear witness against me. But they have brought the wrong man: not a jury this side of hell would convict on his word.'

'Why should they not,' I asked, 'if he is on the side of the rich men?'

'There is some honour left in the land,' was the answer. 'Juries have refused to convict before if they thought badly of the witnesses. No, they would have to bring someone better than a paid assassin against me, and that will not be so easy. Those who would have spoken have been discredited, and those who have kept their honour will never speak, never!'

He took me by the arm.

'Remember that, never forget it. There are thousands, aye and tens of thousands, who held each other's lives in their hands but who never spoke; no, not though they were threatened and bribed. Ignorant men they were, men of no learning, but their hearts were great.'

For a while he paused, the blood left his face and the passion his voice.

'But I have not been idle either. Some of those who have come here these past weeks are men known to me from long ago. I have made my own enquiries and it may be that Cranley himself has a past better hidden. I am waiting now on news and if it should be what I think, then Cranley may wish he had stayed hidden in hell, or wherever he came from.'

He rose at that and we went up the stairs together. As we parted on the landing he said that which surprised me. My father, you know, was as just and kind a man as ever lived, but he was not one to wear his heart on his sleeve, being in that a true man of the moors, and so I was surprised when he put his hand on my shoulder, and taken aback by what he said:

'It hurts me for you not to have a new coat, and to see you walking about in rags.'

Before I could answer he went quickly to his room, and I, slowly, to mine.

CHAPTER TEN

For the next few days we saw no more of Fletcher, nor of the mysterious Castle, but I saw much of Cranley. The reason for this was that Bloom was spending a great deal of time at the new mill, preparing for the steam-engines. This threw me into Cranley's company often. He could not forbear from making jeering remarks about the great demonstration—references to sore feet leading to sore heads—but, true to Fletcher's advice, he did try to be more jocular with me, although in such a heavy-handed and forced manner a dog would have mistrusted him. Now it was all Daniel this, and Daniel that, and what a good lad I was, and what a good master I had. For such an uncouth, illiterate man, Cranley had a great belief in words. I bore this with as much patience as I could, but my mind was fixed on one thing only: the date of our great meeting—the ninth of August.

And then, just eight days before the date fixed, word came from Manchester that the magistrates had banned the meeting! The weavers gathered in the Robin Hood in a mood of great consternation and there was much wild talk about going, whether the magistrates wished it or not. Cranley strutted about with a wicked grin for a day or so, but then news came that Orator Hunt had called a fresh meeting, one the magistrates could not ban. And so it was the weavers who were perked and Cranley's face slipped into its natural expression of vile bad temper.

The new meeting, as I suppose all know, was set for the sixteenth of August, Anno Domini 1819. As James Adshead pointed out, this delay was in our favour, for it gave us time to perfect our drilling and to win over those few weavers who were still doubtful of the justice of our cause. Once or twice father, and others, went over to Heytop, to see if the Saints had decided to come or no, but each time they found them in prayer, no word having come as yet from the Holy Spirit.

Wild rumours were spread about in those days. There were tales that the King's Guard had marched up from London. Stories that the inhabitants of Manchester, fearing that the place was to be destroyed, had fled the town and that now it was an empty desolation with only wild dogs roaming the street, as Moscow was said to have been when Napoleon entered it in his war with the Russian Tsar. But to all these stories father turned a deaf ear.

'Such tales are always told before any great event,' he said. 'Let us not mind them but go quietly about our business that, when we march, we will do so knowing that we are sensible men going about a sensible affair.'

And so we did. The women cooked and washed and the men worked at the loom or took their scythes to the grazing, for it was August now and the mowing was upon us.

Once or twice I tried to sound out Bloom about the March, and Reform, but he showed no interest.

'It's a weavers' battle,' he said, 'none of mine, or yours either. You are an engineer now. But I will say this. The world has to change, and change it will. But the new machines will do it, not all this mithering about going to Manchester. Them weavers up there won't be needed when steam gets here. I wish them no ill-will, but it's the truth. Tell your father I said so, and tell him that I'm surprised that a sensible fellow like him is getting involved in it.'

I protested at this but Bloom brushed me aside.

'He set you to working at this trade, didn't he? What did he do that for if he didn't see the writing on the wall?'

When I went home that night I was thoughtful and wished to tell father what Bloom had said. Father was unusually cheerful when I got in the house. While I had my dinner, he stood on the doorstep in his shirt-sleeves and smoked a pipe, cracking jokes with people passing by as if the good old days were back. When I had finished eating, he would not let me speak but told me to put my coat on and come for a stroll. I was glad enough to do this for it was a fine evening, and to stroll through it with father was a great a pleasure as I could wish.

We sauntered off through the dusk, having a crack with the neighbours as we passed them, and went onto the moor. There we sat watching the lights of scattered cottages and farms begin to glow, while small white moths came to rest on our jackets, as lightly as snow-flakes. I told father what Bloom had said. To my surprise he did not disagree.

'It is true. Steam will change us, and our way of life. The question, is will it change it for the worse or for the better? To be sure, if we do not make our voice heard then it will be for the worse.'

He said this easily and lightly, as if he were well content with the world. When I observed on this, he chuckled.

'I am, too. More content tonight than I have been for many a day. John called here today, do you mind him?'

Some of the pleasure of the evening ebbed away when I heard John's name mentioned, but I said that I did remember him.

'Aye, he called today, but not alone. He brought with him a man; one who has seen the inside of a gaol.'

He turned on his elbow and stared at me. 'You do not like such men, Daniel, I know that well enough. But because a man has been in gaol does not mean he is bad, and that a man has no home or family is not a sign that he does not want one. But no matter. This one who came today was gaoled in 1803 for speaking treason. He says that he never was a traitor but that a witness was brought against him who lied, and that he was convicted because of those lies. Some five years later, while he was serving his sentence in Stafford Gaol, he saw a strange thing. He saw the witness who had lied against him walking the felons' wards. It seems that this liar had been convicted of forgery and only escaped hanging because the government had stepped in as a reward for his spying and his lying.'

The light had drained entirely from the sky now and father's face was merely a pale blur. He took hold of my arm and the grip of his fingers was like pincers.

'Do you know who that man was, Daniel? Do you know who it was that perjured himself, who forged banknotes, who walked the felons' cell in Stafford Gaol?'

I hardly needed the telling but I let father speak. It was not for me to spoil his triumph.

'It was Master Cranley, Daniel. That dog, he who would clap irons on my legs, has worn them on his own! And his name, Daniel, Cranley's name, has been whispered across half England. Not the genteel half, but the one where memories are long and friendships true. And now I have him in the palm of my hand. You see he has been a gaol-bird and not a gentleman in England will speak to him once that has been made known. He will be like a leper and, in the end, he will have to go. And though he swear himself black and blue not even Judge Jeffreys would accept his word. And now we may go home and sleep sound.'

He rose from the moor, black against the sky.

'I have said before that the past climbs from its grave, though it be buried never so deep. Now I see that it is well to live your life in such a way that it is unspotted by shame.'

CHAPTER ELEVEN

Few days remained now before the March and each was marked by a special quality. My fears of Cranley had gone since father told me his news and I went down into the Clough in a mood of bold self-confidence.

With the edge of my fears dulled, I threw myself at my work with new energy. There was much work to be done for Bloom went to Birmingham to see the engines brought safely up the canals. However there was nothing I did not feel capable of tackling. I even made a small improvement to one of the machines which made it easier to handle. It was a slight thing, to be sure, but it was my own idea and gave me a thrill of creation such as I had never felt before. Cranley gave out that this was a great brain-child, worthy of an Arkwright, and promised to give me half-a-crown. The money never materialised, but something else did.

The day before the March, when I was busy at my bench, Cranley called me. He took me into his counting-house and, turning out a poor wisp of a thing he had taken to calling his clerk, he produced a bottle of brandy and two glasses. I wondered who the other glass was for and was amazed when it was pressed on me. I refused it, for I was forbidden to touch ardent spirits. Cranley was angry at this but hid his wrath.

'Well then,' he said, 'you shall have a mug of good ale.'

I refused that, too, whereupon Cranley offered to have a pot of tea made. I could hardly say no to that, and when the clerk had mashed the tea, we sat down together, I as amazed as if I was in the King's palace, drinking tea with him.

Cranley supped his grog and gave me a knowing look.

'There now,' he said. ' 'Tis not so bad at Cranley's after all, is it?'

I mumbled a vague reply and Cranley gave me a grin as rotten as old twill.

'I suppose you will be wanting the day off tomorrow, to go a-marching with the weavers?'

I did want the next day off, but whether Cranley intended giving it to me or not was indifferent to me, for I was going to go whatever he thought.

'Well,' Cranley said. 'You can have the day off—and I will only dock you half a day's wages, for you have worked well this past few weeks. There now!' and he leaned back as if he had given me the Open Sesame to Ali Baba's cave.

I hummed over this and Cranley took a swig of his brandy.

'Many people say bad things about me, Daniel. I know that. But I do not care. Sticks and stones may break my bones but names will never hurt me. That is my motto and be damned to those who think otherwise!'

I did not know what to say to this surprising outburst and contented myself with staring into my tea-pot.

'Remember what I say, Daniel,' Cranley continued. 'Those who call me names are envious of my good fortune. They are those who cannot work as I have done and make a success of their lives.' He gave me a fawning look. 'Now you, lad, you will go far in the land. Any fool can see that. But I dare say there are those who call you such names as they call me.'

'It may be so,' I muttered uneasily, for suspicions had fallen on me and my father when I first went to the mill. Cranley leaned back and lighted his dirty old pipe.

'To make your way in the world you need friends, though. You have seen the gentlemen who have called in here at the mill?'

I said that I had and Cranley nodded. 'You would, you have a head on your shoulders. Those gentlemen are rich men, magistrates and such, like the one who was here when I gave you all the day off when you hurt your head. They are rich men, but they wish to get richer—and they come to me to see that they do! They are my friends, Daniel.'

He poured out more brandy and swigged it.

'Bloom will be back soon with the machinery for the new mill: then I will have a factory here that will be the wonder of this valley, and you will be at work on that wonder. Many a father would give good money to have his lad trained in the working of the steam-engines. They are a power which will change the world, and nothing will stop them coming. A man who understands them will make money, as much as he could wish for, and he will be his own master, aye, that he will.'

Then he gave me a sideways look, such a one as the Devil might have given Jesus when tempting him with the kingdoms of this world.

'Think of that when the weavers moan around you next. Why, come twenty years, and there will not be a hand-weaver left. They will be in the mills, every last one of them—those that we choose to set to work.'

Although I said nothing to this, it made me angry. That the weavers should be forced from their homes and made to toil in the mills under dogs such as Cranley was a bitter thought. True it was no more than my father had said but that made it no better in my ears. Indeed, that Cranley should echo the words seemed a kind of blasphemy. I suppose it was the relish with which he spoke, his air of evil anticipation, that made his words so repugnant.

Then Cranley changed his tone. He leaned forward confidentially.

'Have you talked with your father about the new machines?'

Of course I answered that I had—how could I not? The whole valley talked about them. I think it was partly the fact that they were coming which had brought some of the weavers on the March.

'Now what does your father think of them?' Cranley went on. 'I would be interested to know.'

I paused before answering. My father said a great deal about them, but I doubted if Cranley would wish to hear it.

'He says that they will bring great changes,' I said, as casually as I could.

'Aye,' Cranley puffed away for a moment. 'Of course, he, being a hand-weaver, will not like the machines. Does he say that?'

'No,' I lied.

'I would,' Cranley said, with an air of great frankness. 'They might take away his livelihood. It would be natural for him to dislike them—maybe to curse them, and their owners. Does he do a bit that way, like?'

I matched Cranley's air of frankness. 'No, he does not curse anyone; and I work at the machines myself, do you see, so it would be like cursing me.'

Cranley pulled his face at that and then tried again.

'You have no mother, Daniel?'

I said I had none and at his question I felt my temper rise a little. It was bad enough to hear my father's name on his lips— to hear my mother's was truly disgusting.

'Neither have I.' Cranley said, pulling his face. Nor father either. I was orphaned when I was a suckling babe.'

I realised then that his turned down mouth was an attempt to show grief and I all but laughed in his face, for I believed him to be as incapable of sorrow as one of his machines.

'If you have no mother, then you will be close to your father.' Cranley did not wait for an answer. 'He will be your best friend with your mother gone. Many a fine talk you will have with him, for he is a fine man, a fine man. You do have many a talk, eh?'

'Yes,' I said, and indeed I could say little else. It was not likely that I would live with my own father and not talk to him.

'I am glad to hear it.' Cranley grunted. 'Your Dad is a good man, one of the old breed. But even the best of men can find himself among evil company.'

I was ready to protest at this but was given no chance.

'Why,' Cranley said, 'I have fallen amongst evil men myself once. Yes, that I have!'—he said this as if the thought would astound me—'And I might have stayed among them but that good men came and took me from their company. You see what that has done for me. I am master of mine own mill and can take men on or turn them off as I please. And when those times come that I have told you of, when we are masters of this vale, it will be well to have me and my like as friends, and ill to have us as enemies. But to have a friend, you must show yourself worthy of friendship.'

He paused for a moment to let this sink in. I looked out of the window. Through it I could see the water-wheel lunging around, and beyond that the blank walls of the mill. Above their blankness it was just possible to see tree-tops swaying and, even beyond them, the grey-green smudge of the moors. The wheel made its usual pleasant gurgle and the machines muttered away, harsh, unceasing, unyielding.

'And has your father talked to you about his travels yet?' Cranley asked, and his voice was no longer false.

'No,' I said, and then I changed my mind. At first, you know, I had made no more of Cranley's babble than I would have of the ravings of a Tom-a-Bedlam, but now—had I been older and wiser I would just have sat there keeping my tongue still and my ears wagging—but now I could bear his voice no longer.

'Yes,' I said. 'He has told me something.'

The change in Cranley was like magic. He crashed his glass to the table and leaned forward as intent as a terrier at a rat hole.

'Where?' he demanded. 'Where has he been?'

I waited for a moment, savouring what I thought might be my triumph.

'Well, he tells me that he has been in Stafford.'

Cranley's face altered as though by magic. The oily smirk went and his ugly face set in his frightening, flat stare.

'Stafford?' he said.

'Why yes, he has walked by Stafford Gaol.'

'When did he say this?' Cranley's voice was thick with an animal growl. The man was showing through the mask, and he was no better than a brute after all.

'He has spoken of it, that is all. I do not remember when.'

With that I made for the door but Cranley was there before me. He grabbed my arm, and the power of his grip took me by surprise.

'What has he told you about Stafford?'

'Let go of me,' I demanded, and wriggled my arm.

'You will go when I let you.' Cranley's face was blacker than the hobs of hell. 'Speak, damn you.'

'I am not standing here to talk about my father to you.' And I am ashamed to say that, bold though my words were, my voice trembled.

Cranley shook me. 'You will talk to me as I tell you. Do you hear?'

'You can't make me,' I cried. 'Nor ten like you.'

'Why,' said Cranley, 'I will break you in pieces—and your damned father with you.'

I tore my arm free from his grip.

'That would be the wish of a dog like you, but you will be beaten at that—'

Before I could finish Cranley cracked me across the face. I staggered backwards and banged against the door. In turn I struck out, missing my target by a mile. Then I was grabbed by the collar and pulled. It was Burns and, as I stumbled, he kicked me and sent me sprawling on the floor.

Cranley came across the room at me and for a moment I feared that I was to be kicked to death on the flag-stones, but he restrained himself.

'Out!' he bawled. 'Get out or I will beat thee so that thy damned father will not recognise thee. Get him off my mill,' he ordered Burns. 'And see that he does not come back.'

Burns tapped me with his clog.

'Tha heard what Master said. Clear off.'

There was nothing for it but to do as I was told. I got my coat and trudged off home, my hands skinned and my tail between my legs. And it was a long way home that night, I may tell you.

My father took my tale with more composure than I had hoped for.

'It helps in a way. For sure Cranley would not have been so savage had there been nothing to this Stafford tale. Having a hint of it now will give him a sleepless night or two, anyway, and there is nothing that he can do against us. We will wait until after the March and then find you another job. Then I will call on Master Cranley. He will be sorry that he struck you, that is sure.'

And so saying he turned again to his loom, but although he worked as smoothly and deftly as ever, and the shuttle flew backwards and forwards as if it had a mind of its own, yet, when I caught a glimpse of his face through the healds of the loom it was as cold and hard as stone.

CHAPTER TWELVE

What with the row with Cranley, and the thought of the next day, I did not think that I would sleep that night. For a long time I lay awake, thinking of the morrow; of the sight of countless weavers and the blare of bands, of the day that would mean a new dawn for us all. But at last I did sleep, to dream of giant fire-engines with Cranley shovelling whole trees into the furnace. Why trees I do not know.

I woke to the sound of a drum throbbing in the street. It seemed to me to be calling the village to rise and dress in its Sunday best, to raise the great banner, and to march behind the trumpet and the drum; down from the hills and moors, through the meadows and the fields where the rushing waters ran; down to the town of Manchester, to the fields of St. Peter where, in order and in peace, with fellowship and goodwill, we would make our just demands known, and light a light for the oppressed of the land.

And so the village met outside the Robin Hood. As we formed into our ranks I looked at the faces of the men; at James Adshead, Tom Spencer, Henry Rowley, Sam Teller; and I felt proud to be in such company, so decent they seemed to me, decent and simple and honourable.

To much good-natured chaff a few stragglers came down from the hills but, to our regret, there was no sign of the Saints. We wished them in, you know. They would have swelled our numbers and made a bolder show, and we felt a certain human sympathy for them. They were weavers, after all.

However, we could wait no longer. Father took his place at the head of the men and raised his stick, James Adshead blew a clear, true note on his trumpet, Sam banged the drum, the flowing banner was raised, and, to a shout of triumph, we set out at last.

The whole village walked out along the pike but at Fenner's Clough those women who were staying to look after the children bade us farewell. Old Caleb urged us to rally behind the Prince,

for he was more confused now than ever. I kissed Emma, who was to be minded by Mrs. Adshead, and promised to bring her a present from Manchester. Then we gave Cranley and his mill three hearty groans and pressed on.

Our drummer kept up a hearty rhythm and we chattered excitedly, but after a while we fell into a quieter mood. It was only just past the crack of dawn, with the world silent and still. The valley was white with mist from the river and there was not a soul to be seen stirring. The silence and emptiness began to have its effect on us: the drum faltered, its sharp, cheery taps slowing into a melancholy beat more suited to a funeral, and finally it stopped altogether. The men began to look at each other from the corners of their eyes, as if they were furtively estimating each other's determination, wondering whether we were the only weavers who had answered the call for Reform and, if so, what would happen to us if the magistrates were out.

Despite these fears we tramped on until we came to the road which runs down to Ban Bridge. There is a spring there and we paused to drink. As we slaked our thirst, we heard a strange wailing noise, as melancholy as the cry of a curlew. It came from the moors, but although we turned and scanned the skyline there was nothing to be seen.

'What might that be?' asked someone.

And then again came the cry. Someone whispered that it might be dragoons. At that the men set their faces tight and gripped their sticks. Father told us to form a line in front of the women and to be ready to use our banner-poles to hold off the horses, should the soldiers try to jostle us.

We stood in an uneasy group listening to the noise, which grew louder. What its cause might be we could not imagine, for it bore no relation to any sound we had heard before. Then, on the crest of the moor, a dark line of men appeared.

'Stand firm,' cried father, and firm we were as the figures moved towards us. But, sheepishly, our sticks were lowered. The people coming towards us were the Saints, led by Obadiah Briggs, and singing Psalms.

Briggs shambled through the bents and held his hands aloft.

'We have spent our days and nights in prayer,' he shouted. 'And last night the Holy Ghost came to us with the message that it would not be against the Lord's will for us to march with thee to Manchester.'

We looked at him in silence and with something of the embarrassment a weak-stomached man might feel looking at a deformity of nature for, although none of us from Helmshaw would have passed for a well-fed farmer, the Saints looked like living scarecrows. They were so gaunt that the bones stuck out of them, their clothes were mere rags, scarcely decent, and their faces had a deadly white look such as I had only seen before on corpses.

Father coughed. 'Well, that is news, good news. You are welcome to march with us. Aye, welcome.'

Briggs' eyes rolled a little and he licked his lips.

'We have prayed for deliverance. We have searched the heavens for a sign, and then, this morning, it seemed to us that we heard a drum rolling and a trumpet call, and it seemed to us that it was that sign which we had called for.'

He looked at us anxiously, as if asking for an assurance that it was so, and there was none among us who would have denied him.

Father waved his hand in an odd gesture and spoke again in a manner curiously irresolute for one so direct:

'We are glad to have you with us—make no mistake of that —but . . . Manchester . . . it is a good step you know . . . all of fourteen miles . . . yes, a good step, eh?' He looked at Briggs almost shyly. 'We have some bread and cheese . . . '

'Bread and cheese?' Briggs muttered. 'Oh aye! We have been fasting, fasting. We have been mortifying the sinful flesh that our actions be not tainted with greed nor covetousness. Thou shalt not covet, says the Lord thy God!'

Father seemed nonplussed by this. 'Aye,' he said vaguely, and shrugged. The shrug was taken up by the other men who looked at each other, raising their eyebrows as if to say, what could be done? But one of the women bustled forward.

'The Holy Ghost won't carry thee to Manchester,' she said stoutly. 'Tha need food in thy bellies. Get this down thee.' And she thrust a half a loaf and a hunk of cheese in Briggs' hands.

Briggs stared at the food intently, as if it contained some great mystery.

'I will not eat,' he cried. 'I will not eat until the powers of evil are overthrown. But my flock may eat. Yea, the good shepherd feeds his flock.'

As he spoke his eyes rolled again and the corner of his mouth twitched back, showing his gums. He shoved the food at his followers who had not, it seemed, his vow of mortification for they ate, greedily, and were ready enough to snap up any other crusts offered from our bagging.

We went on then. Behind us the Saints chanted their Psalms and we, too, sang. Ours were old country songs, for we had no taste for religious music, nor did we know any songs of rebellion. Now on the road we began to meet other people, marching like us. They had banners of their own, many wore white 'liberty-hats', and some of them had leaves in their hats, which stood for the laurel wreath of victory. This delicate touch had not occurred to us but, not to be outdone in anything we could do, we broke off sprigs of hawthorn and wore those.

The mists of the morning were blowing away now, and all across the valley we could see groups of people marching. The sun illumined banners and glinted on instruments of brass and the clear air was full of the sound of the trumpet and the fife. By the time we had reached Tottington the road was thronged with marchers and our fears of the early dawn seemed ridiculous. All the world was marching; what force, be it ne'er so malevolent, could withstand us?

By six of the morning we were going down the long hill of Walmsley into Bury. I was walking at the head of the column, light-footed and light-hearted, when, down the hill, I saw a cloud of dust hanging in the summer sky.

At first I thought that it might be arising from earlier marchers, but as we drew near we came upon a team of horses drawing a huge cart. There were eight horses, great animals twice my height and aglitter with brass and copper, their manes threaded with red and white ribbon as if it were May Day. They threw up their heads as we passed, as though in greeting, and we got a greeting too from their driver, who raised his whip in salute. A half-mile further down the road we came upon another team and cart, and on the outskirts of Bury, another. As it went past someone called to us and looking up we saw Bloom.

He scrambled off the cart and came to us. After we had exchanged 'good days', he asked us if we were going to the meeting. Those who heard gave a resounding 'aye!' but Bloom's face was longer than usual.

'We have come through there with the machines from Watt and B.' he waved at the cart. 'Manchester is full of troops. There are two regiments of infantry, the Hussars, and artillery! They have called out the Yeomanry and the magistrates are sitting. They have put up notices telling all the people to stay away from the meeting.'

'Why,' said father, 'they may say what they wish but the meeting is within the law. We walk peacefully and without arms on a lawful errand. Why should they call out the troops?'

Bloom shook his head dolefully. 'You think that you are going to a peaceful meeting, but what you think and what the magistrates think are two different things. You be careful.'

Father thanked Bloom for this news but it was plain that he took little heed of it. Instead he asked whether Bloom had seen many more marchers.

'That I have,' came the answer. 'We came up the canals through Cheshire last night and there were hundreds gathering. It looked as if all the world and his wife were out.' He looked at us shrewdly. 'It may be that is the reason why the magistrates are alarmed. They would not be afraid of a small group, but when there are many gathered, then they become frightened —and frightened dogs bite.' He paused then, as if wondering whether to speak further. 'I do not wish to alarm you, but last night I was drinking at an inn in Manchester; a Yeoman was there, and he boasted that his company had had their swords new ground and that they were as sharp as razors. He said that they were going to hack the Radicals to pieces. He was drunk, I should say that.'

Father looked grave, but resolute too. 'That may be so, but the man was drunk you say. I do not think there is any need to fear. There will be many thousands standing there in the light of day. We are not in Poland to be cut down by drunken shopkeepers, but in England in the nineteenth century. What you heard was idle boasting by one who wished he could brag of being at Waterloo. But thank you for the warning.' He hesitated and then clapped his hand on Bloom's shoulder.

'You are a good man, Bloom, and you have done well by my lad here. Why not come with us? We go to stand for your rights too.'

Bloom was firm. 'No, it is your fight, the weavers. But I wish you well. It gives me no pleasure to see men treated like dogs. Take care.'

With that he shook hands all round and shambled after the waggons—but not before he had seized my arm: 'Steam!' he hissed! 'It's all on those carts!'

And then we parted, he with the machines up the long hill to Cranley's works, we with our banners and drums, down to Manchester.

CHAPTER THIRTEEN

I have heard it said, since those days, that those who marched on Manchester were a rabble. Those who speak thus could not have seen the Bury Union. We drew up in the market square a thousand strong and our leaders marched down the ranks like colonels. Those they deemed drunk, or troublesome, were ordered out of the lines and told to find their way to Manchester by themselves. When the leaders got to us, they admired our banner but told us to leave aside our sticks, as they might be regarded as weapons by the Manchester constables.

We demurred at this. 'Why,' said James, 'we have been told that the troops and Yeomanry are out in the town. Are we to have no means of defence?'

Grigg, the leader of the Bury Union, was firm.

'No one is going to attack us, but carrying sticks might appear that we wish for trouble. Throw them aside or fall out.'

At that we threw our sticks away. Then Grigg stood before the marchers and addressed us. He told us that we were marching for justice and freedom and that we must show ourselves worthy of it. He commanded us to walk quietly and to obey our captains in all things, then no harm could come to us and the day would be remembered with pride forever. He began then to remind us of the ills we had undergone and the hardships we had suffered, but the crowd became restless.

'Let us get on our way,' they cried, and it was plain that all there knew everything Grigg could tell about hardship or why were they there? Like a sensible man Grigg accepted this.

'Very well,' he cried. 'Let us march! Three cheers for justice!'

This we gave heartily and three more for Mr. Hunt, and then, to a rousing tune from the Bury band, we left the square.

It was a brilliant morning by now. The sun struck down but there was a light wind to temper the heat, and I enjoyed the walk. At every hamlet there were people waiting to cheer us; at Radcliffe and Stand, Polefield and Whitefield. There were less at Heaton, for the Earl of Wilton held that place and few dared come out lest they incur his wrath; but there were windows dressed in fresh boughs and white ribbon for all that. Across the meadows of the deer-park we could see the great hall where the Earl lived, and heartily we booed it, for what were earls and lords to the bold weavers of the moors?

Our village held together well, but the Saints felt the weight of the miles on their famished legs. Some few of them had fallen out and the others shuffled along, more like candidates for a sick-club than Radical Reformers. Only Briggs marched on tirelessly, with a high prancing walk, his eyes like coals in the whiteness of his face. Our men spoke to him now and then but he never answered. Only occasionally he shouted incoherently at the remnants of his flock, but I doubt whether they understood him.

On we went to Crumpsall and there a vast procession led the way. This was the Middleton Union, led by Bamford himself. Him I saw marching along under a blue and white banner. Behind them was the Saddleworth Union led by Doctor Healey. They, too, had a banner and a dismal one it was, more fitted for a funeral than ought else, for it was black with what appeared to be a painted dagger, and had the words 'Equal Representation or Death' daubed over it.

There was some frowning in our column at this gloomy emblem since it bore a threatening air which marred the festive nature of the day. But it was not for us to tell another Union what it might carry and so we proceeded without comment to Mr. Johnson's cottage at Smedley where our speaker, Mr. Hunt, was waiting to be escorted into the town. There was some delay here for the 'Orator', as he was known, was not quite ready. We took the opportunity to rest ourselves in the meadows. Although we idled in the sweet grass, Briggs never sat down but walked before the Saints, to and fro, to and fro, muttering to himself in a strange babble. He talked of Sehon and Og, and how they had been slain by the hand of the Lord, great Kings though they had been, and of how the cities of the plain, Sodom and Gomorrah, had been utterly destroyed. His wife, a sensible, plain body, called to him to come and rest, but he paid her no more heed than he would a fly and continued walking through the grass in his strange, loping way.

After a while it seemed that Mr. Hunt was ready. We rose from the ground and the thousands with us rose too. The thought came to me that when the children of Israel rose to follow Moses from the yoke of the Pharaohs, they must have cut a similar figure: men, women, and children, all groaning under bondage but seeing a new light and all, whatever their differences might be, rising in a common purpose and going to their Promised Land—for such Manchester seemed to me that morning.

Our leaders moved forward and we followed. At the bar of the Parish of Manchester there was a troop of dragoons, ready for trouble I have no doubt, but all they got from us was a cheery 'good morning', repeated a thousand times. Beyond the bar the River Irk has cut a deep cleft. There are two roads there: one leads through the cleft but the other runs above the river, through Collyhurst. Where the roads separate the procession halted for some little time. I was impatient and slipped forward to find out what was causing the delay, and, also, I was mad keen to see the great Hunt at close quarters.

Hunt was in a carriage with other gentlemen, looking down on Bamford and one or two other men. He cut a fine figure for he was tall and handsome, although somewhat haughty, and he wore a white top hat. He seemed rather angry and was speaking pretty sharply to Bamford. He, however, was holding his ground and looked quite resolute. It seemed that Hunt wished the whole March to go down the cleft whereas Bamford chose to lead us along the top road.

'I do not like the thought of us going down by the river,' he said. 'If there should be any misdeeds by the authorities then we would be in a bad way down there. It is better for us to take the high road.'

Hunt, rather red in the face at the challenge to his authority, did not like this. But whether he liked it or not Bamford cared little. Hunt looked around in a bad-tempered way but found no support from those around Bamford. Why it was easy to see. Hunt was the great man, right enough, but Bamford was our leader—tried and true—and his word was good enough for us.

So, after a certain cold exchange of civilities, we parted. Hunt and his party into the cleft, we along the high road.

Although we had lost some of our numbers by this parting we made a fine sight as we went along but, after a while, Bamford seemed to have a change of heart and we went into the valley after all. Although it was but a short step from there to our rallying point, by parting we had lost touch with Hunt and managed to lose our way. Instead of going across Hanging Ditch into Deansgate, we wandered up Market Street to the place they call Piccadilly and found that we must turn down Moseley Street to reach the meeting.

I was a little awed by the town; not by its size, for it did not seem enormous, nor by its streets, which were mean rather than otherwise, but by the workshops which loomed everywhere. They were like giant fortresses, or prisons, in which every convict served a life sentence. And yet their size was, in a way, comforting. Before that day Cranley had seemed to me the very type of our overlords and his mill a bastion of injustice, but compared with the vast factories and warehouses of Manchester, and the merchant princes who owned them, he shrank into insignificance, seeming no more than a petty tyrant after all. And thinking that made me reflect that perhaps the men who commanded these mills were no more than Cranley, no more than men after all, no more than I.

These thoughts ran through my head as we idled in Moseley Street in the shade of its tall houses. The windows were full of ladies and gentlemen who stared down at us as curiously as if we were savages from the Ivory Coast. We stared back as inquisitively but that, it seemed, was not the proper thing to do. One gentleman shouted down at us that we had no breeding! I think, though, that the people in the house were afraid of us, for he was hastily pulled away and another man appeared who gave us a nervous smile, as if to apologise.

While we were amusing ourselves in this fashion, a cry came from the head of the column and we rose to our feet. Ahead of us, the drums throbbed and the trumpets called, their long notes echoing off the walls. The banners of our Clubs rose into the air like great birds on outspread wings, and behind them we marched around a tall church and onto the fields of St. Peters.

CHAPTER FOURTEEN

As we entered the field there was a cheer, coming from the throats of more thousands than I can tell. As much as anything about that day I remember the sound. There was nothing in it to frighten: nothing of anger or hatred, violence or war, but only a cry of exultant welcome. For think how many there that day had risen at dawn in remote hamlets and bothies and formed up behind their banners, wondering what the day would bring; wondering, as we had done, whether they would be alone and at the mercy of their masters, but who had trusted in the words of a few men, mere weavers like themselves, and had faced their task boldly and held true to their word. Think of that and then think how they, and we, felt at the sight of that vast gathering—for vast it was. Think of that, and be humble.

For our part we answered the shout of the crowd lustily. As we went amongst them, we raised the cry that we, the weavers, used on that day. 'Order,' we cried, 'Order,' and the crowd took it up in a steady chant, 'Order, Order, Order,' and I understood that it was not a command imposed on us by our leaders, but a promise that sprang from our confidence and strength.

The marshals led us to our appointed place, which, to my disappointment, was on the edge of the crowd, by a row of houses. Although I stood on tiptoe I could see little but the back of men's necks. However James and father heaved me up so that I could have a general view of the field. At the far side, away from us, there was a row of carts, decorated with blue and white, and bright with banners. Those were the hustings where the speakers were to stand when they arrived, for the Orator had not yet appeared. Satisfied that I had seen what there was to see, I asked to be let down. But as I was lowered, I saw something strange. By the side of the houses I caught sight of a flash of light, as if it came from metal, but bright metal, as if it might be a sword. I saw no more than a wink of light but it was disturbing, ominous, like a flash of lightning across a sultry, day-time sky.

On the ground again I looked about me. As yet there was no one behind us and I could see the houses at the edge of the field clearly. Drawn up before them was a line of men, not weavers, and the windows of the houses were full of men, some in uniform. But whatever had caused the flash of metal was not in sight. I called father's attention to the line of men and he spoke to someone nearby who told us that they were police constables, and that all the magistrates of Manchester and Salford were gathered in the houses under Rev. Hulton.

'They have come to see their defeat then,' joked father. 'I am told that they tried to ban this meeting.'

'Aye,' came the answer. 'But they might as well have tried to ban it from raining when it wished. I tell you—'

But what the friendly stranger might have told us I never did find out for from a distance we heard a band strike up, and then a storm of applause.

'It's Hunt!' James cried, and gave an ear-splitting 'huzza!'

Nothing would do me then, of course, but that I should be heaved up again to see the great man make his triumphal entry. He was in his carriage but there were no horses in the shafts. They had been unyoked and he was drawn by men—willingly. He stood up so that all might see him and waved his white hat at the people. I saw him clearly, tall, erect, handsome, and with something of a smile of pleasure on his lips at his welcome, for he was a man who liked the plaudits. He was then taken to the hustings and I dropped down. The crowd fell silent, for the speech, but we had to wait a little.

'What is happening?' I asked James, who was a long fellow and well able to see over the crowd.

'They are moving the hustings for some reason,' he answered.

Once more there was a delay and then there came an ear-splitting roar. Hunt had risen. The roar went on for a full ten minutes and when it did fade away there was a dead silence. It was hard to believe that such a crowd could be so quiet, and yet such was the hush that I heard a baby whimper, although it was on the other side of the field from us. Then came Hunt's voice.

'My friends,' he said. 'We are gathered—' and then came a groan from the people behind us. We turned and saw the constables coming into the crowd. At their head was a big, sour-faced fellow, with a determined air about him.

'Make way there,' he cried. 'Give way in the name of the Law!'

He was waving a roll of paper, and his manner was such that the crowd made way for him, although not without some muttering. As he strode through the people, the constables with him formed a double line through the crowd, making a kind of corridor.

'What's happening then?' asked father.

The man he had spoken to earlier turned to us.

'Why, that fellow is Joe Nadin. He's the Deputy Constable of the town and those men are his assistants. And if you ask me, that paper he has is a warrant!'

James then called to us:

'He is at the hustings talking to Mr. Hunt.' Then he gave a startled cry: 'Why, look here!'

He pointed behind us. We turned and our jaws dropped. Coming into the crowd was a squadron of the Yeoman Cavalry!

Much has been written about that day. Words by, I suppose, the million have been written of it, men have argued, lied and fought over it, and some have spent long months in gaol because of it. But, although some say this and others that, and although they might be men of great position and property or education, if their words contradict mine then I can only say that I was there, and that I write of what I saw, confused and cloudy though that was.

No one on the field was much disturbed by the appearance of Nadin and his men. They were interrupting our proceedings but they were on foot and unarmed, and they were dressed in ordinary citizens' clothes. But the cavalry—they were a different kettle of fish. I have said how hateful men on horseback had come to seem to me—and not to me alone. Judge how we felt then when we saw these horsemen come trotting into our field. Remember, too, that they were not regular soldiers, who did their work, however dirty, in no sort of malice, but the Yeomanry, volunteer shopkeepers and employers, led by the landlords:

men who kept over our heads the threat of homelessness and want, men who took from our mouths the bread we earned by the sweat of our brows, men actuated by personal hatreds—and half of them drunk. It would have been a matter of no surprise if we had seized them from their chargers and thrown them into the dust. But we held firm. None among us raised a fist against them and they went down the line of Nadin's police as safely as lambs in a fold.

I see them now, stiff in their gaudy uniforms of blue and white, their harness jingling like little bells. Their sabres glinted in the sunlight but their faces were shadowed by their tall hats so that there was no sign of humanity about them. A captain led them, swinging his shadowed head from side to side, as if daring any dog there to bark. Next to him rode a bugler with a silver trumpet and a pennant with the colours of the squadron fluttering from it. M.Y.C. was on the flag. The Manchester Yeoman Cavalry.

The crowd stared at them mutely as they moved among us, those nearest the troops coughing a little as the fine dust stirred by the horses drifted towards them. The dust settled on the faces of the people, making them appear masked, robbing them, too, of life and animation, while above them moved the jingling horses, the gaudy uniforms, and the bright twinkling brass.

We were as still as dolls for a moment, then from the hustings there came an angry roar. 'They are arresting Hunt!' we heard. We stared at each other amazed. How could they arrest our leader? But then we heard worse than roars, we heard screams!

James peered over the crowd and gave an amazed jerk of his head.

'They are attacking the people!' he cried. 'They are cutting the people!'

There was no need for his news. Over his shoulder we could see the Yeomanry charging their horses at the crowd, their arms swinging and their sabres flashing. Father seized me.

'Come away,' he shouted, and we turned to get free from the people. But at our backs a new line of horsemen were approaching. The people with us tried to run but everywhere, it seemed, there was a horseman charging the crowd. Everywhere people were on the ground, holding gashed heads and arms, or face down in the dust. As the people milled about, it gave more space for the Cavalry, who charged across the field, hacking and slashing, and swearing like madmen. The dust rose like a fog and through the haze the horsemen loomed like giants, and always their arms were swinging, swinging, like flails on the threshing-floor, or reapers in the field.

We ran; jumping over bodies, over the broken banners and the wreckage of the hustings. Away in a corner was a row of cottages with a low wall separating them from the rest of the field. We dodged a Yeoman, who swung a blow at us, and made for this. We were within a dozen yards when a group of horsemen galloped across to us. The leader, seeing that we were fleeing, and that we were but a man and a lad, pulled aside, anxious I suppose for greater glory elsewhere. But as we were at the wall and within a yard of safety, I heard a savage cry.

'Get them,' a voice bellowed. 'Cut them down!' And looking back I saw Cranley!

Immediately a trooper dashed at us, his sword poised for the slash. Father grabbed me and pushed me half over the wall, then stooped and picked up a broken flag-pole. I clambered onto the wall and saw the trooper cut at father. He stood his ground though, and as the soldier loomed over him, he jabbed upwards with the pole and smashed the Yeoman in the ribs, lifting him clear from the saddle. But before he could do anything else, Cranley came at him from the side and slashed him down.

I shouted in anguish as I saw father fall and made to leap back to aid him, but I was caught from behind and dragged over the wall. I fell awkwardly but was saved from a sabre-cut myself, for, as I fell, Cranley drove his horse forward and chopped at me and his sword struck sparks from the stone. I struggled to my feet but was held by a massive fist. I twisted round and saw that I was being held by John.

'My father—' I shouted, trying to wriggle free, but John shook his head.

'You cannot go back there. The troops are out to kill you.' He pressed me back into a group of men who were holding off the soldiers by hurling brick-bats at them and jabbing with banner-poles.

'I will get your Dad. My word on it. Here, take him.'

And taken I was. I was bustled away from the wall and led through a ginnel which ran into a little street, as quiet and peaceful as if it were a thousand miles from the hacking and cutting and terror of the fields. The men I was with held a hasty talk, one of them keeping me secure with a tight grip. After a moment they broke up and sauntered off, hands in pockets, and I was left with one man.

He took my arm, gave me a little shake, and whispered to me urgently, 'You must come with me, it is for your own good.'

I protested feebly, but the man was adamant. 'Your father will be got free. For his sake we must get away. Come. And remember, my name is Luke, Luke Simmons.

I was too dazed to fully understand what was being said to me and I suffered myself to be led away like a child. At the corner of the street there was a gap in the houses. Through it I caught a last glimpse of the fields. A huge cloud of dust hung over them but through the dust I could see, like shadows, the black shapes of the Cavalry as they roamed the ground. By some trick of the light they seemed huge, gigantic, as if to emphasise the greatness of their triumph—and the greatness of our defeat.

CHAPTER FIFTEEN

Luke hustled me up the lane and onto Moseley Street. It was full of people who were fleeing the town as if it had been stricken by plague. We ran with the panic-stricken horde up to Piccadilly. There, regular troops of the Cavalry were guarding the roads which led to Rochdale and Oldham, and the other country towns. They were not obstructing the people but with them were Yeomen and civilians. Occasionally one of these would point out a figure in the crowd and then the troops would move in and seize the person. It was like nothing so much as men dapping for trout.

On seeing this Luke halted and drew back into the shadow of a house. 'Those are informers,' he said. 'If they see me I shall be picked off like a ripe apple. We must try another way, come on.'

He took my arm and we cut down a quiet lane which ran past a bleaching-field and a big spinning-mill. 'We will try crossing the River Medlock,' he said. 'There is a bridge and it may be quiet.'

He held my coat as we hurried along and I needed it, for I was so dazed by the events of the day that, if left alone, I would have sunk to the ground and fallen asleep. I stumbled along as well as I could but at the bridge our way was barred again. A few infantrymen were guarding the crossing and a corporal was turning back all who tried to pass.

'Get up through the town,' he was saying to a dejected group of weavers, and was deaf to all their pleas.

'Well, well,' said Luke, coolly. 'We are boxed in all right. Still, there are other ways.'

We turned and began to make our way back up the lane, but as we reached the mill we saw two men with big sticks turn into the lane from Moseley Street.

'Nadin's crows,' Luke said. 'No way out there,' and he turned into the gateway of the mill as casually as if he were a workman coming back from his dinner. Inside the gateway was a yard, and inside the yard was a cart, laden with yarn, with two horses in the shafts. And on the cart was a man, smoking a pipe.

As we entered, he cocked an eye at us but said nothing. Luke sauntered across to the cart, patted one of the horses on the shoulder, and looked up at the man.

'Good day, friend,' he cried.

The carter stared down as motionless as a wooden idol, which he somewhat resembled, being a gnarly sort of fellow.

'Fine beasts you have here, friend,' said Luke. 'I see you are loaded and ready to go.' He looked up interrogatively at the carter who, for answer, took the pipe from his mouth and spat at Luke's feet.

'Aye, I see you are,' Luke went on, as if he were talking to the friendliest fellow in the world. 'Now, me and my lad here might fancy a ride in your cart. You see, we wish to save our legs. It might be worth a shilling to you.'

At this the carter removed the pipe from his mouth, stared at it for a moment, spat again, and replaced it. 'Eighteen pence,' he said. 'Each.'

Luke appeared to give this some consideration. 'He is only a lad,' he said. 'Ninepence for him, eh?'

The carter reached down, took up the reins, and gave them a jerk. One of the horses clopped a hoof on the cobbles and nodded its head, as if saying that it was ready to go. Luke held up his hand.

'Right you are, friend. Eighteen pence apiece, a fair price, right enough.'

The carter dropped the reins and gave us a careful look. 'Where might you be going?' he asked.

Luke pursed his lips and gave a sideways glance at the yard-gates. 'Well, friend, where might you be going?'

'Mossley,' came the reply, and Luke gave the horse a resounding slap. 'Mossley, now! Just the very place. Yes, a bit of luck for us. We shall be having our dinner soon, lad.' He made to climb on the cart but the carter let his whip fall before him and stuck out his hand.

'Three shillings,' he said.

Somewhat hastily, Luke counted out the money. 'We will ride under the covers if it's all the same to you, friend,' he said. 'Have a nap like, on the way.'

The carter made no objection to this, so we climbed on the cart, the covers were lashed over us, and the cart moved off.

It was roasting hot under the covers, the yarn was soft, and I was so exhausted that my eyes closed the minute I lay down and I fell into an uneasy, trembling doze. I had quick dreams, more like visions than dreams, in which, again and again, huge horsemen loomed over me, slashing with sabres as big as scythe blades, and, over and over, I saw my father fall beneath a cruel slash.

Despite my slumber, I was, I suppose, aware of the swaying of the cart, for I awoke suddenly to find that we had stopped. I gave a whimpering cry but Luke clapped his hand over my mouth. 'Lie still,' he whispered.

I wagged my head and he removed his hand. Outside I could hear voices, one of them sharp and commanding.

'Where are you going?' this voice demanded.

'Mossley,' came our driver's surly reply.

'And what have you in there?' We heard the clatter of a horse, as if the rider was urging it around the cart. We stiffened, expecting to be discovered at any moment.

'Yarn,' said our driver, 'from Mister Arkwright's mill. And I'm late.'

Whether it was the mighty name of Arkwright, our driver's complaint that he was late, or merely the bother of undoing the covers I do not know; but we heard the voice tell the driver to get on, and not to give any lifts to any damned Radicals. The wheels ground around and we swung along, both of us breathing the harder. The horses jogged on and, after a while, the wheels ceased crashing on stone setts, and instead swished through soft sand.

Luke dug me in the ribs. 'We are outside the town, now. We will soon be clear of the troops.'

I do not know that I cared greatly about the news. I felt as if I were in some kind of nightmare, trapped as I was underneath the covers, my mouth parched, and my limbs quivering with nerves and tiredness. It was hard for me to grasp that I was in such a situation and so I tried to push the awareness away and merely lay, inert and supine, staring at the fine pattern of light above me where the sun shone through the canvas, letting the cart take me where it might.

And then, once more, we were stopped by a patrol. A rough voice asked whether we were from Manchester, and when our driver admitted that we were, demanded what he was carrying.

'Yarn for Mister Arkwright's weavers,' came the answer. 'And a man and a lad.'

Luke cursed when he heard that. He tried to claw his way free from the covers but the stout canvas held us as fast as a coffin. And when they were drawn back we found ourselves looking at a circle of Yeomanry.

Their captain was a bully-boy with something of the air of a country butcher about him and who was the worse for drink. 'Out, thee,' he ordered.

We climbed from the cart looking a sorry sight. I was but a lad, and a tired one at that, and Luke was no Samson. We were both covered with lint from the yarn and looked more like two snowmen than two human beings. I think our wretchedness aroused some deep impulse of cruelty in the bully-boy, for he sniggered at us and took out his sabre and swung it under our noses.

'Thou be damned Radical Reformers, bain't thee,' he cried. 'I know thy type.'

Luke tried to put a bold face on matters. 'I don't know what you're talking about,' he said. 'We are weavers and have been to Manchester with our work.'

'Aye,' said the Yeoman, 'and come back hiding in a cart. I know what that means. Thou hast been trying to destroy Parliament!'

'Not a bit of it,' Luke cried in an injured voice. 'We are honest workmen and wished to save our legs a long walk. We paid for our ride. Is that not so?' he appealed to our driver. The carter spat and agreed that we had paid for our drive.

'Well then,' Luke said, as if that disposed of the matter. 'We have a sight further to go yet, so having answered you we shall be off. Come on lad.' And he walked straight at the Yeomen, one of whom began to pull his horse aside to let us pass!

I do believe that Luke's impudence might have done the trick and we would have walked free had it not been for the bully-boy.

'Wait thee,' he growled, and turned to me. 'Who art thou?' he asked.

You must remember that I was worn out by the day and could scarcely stand, let alone think, but I did my best. 'He is my Dad,' I said, pointing to Luke.

When I spoke I saw a little smile creep across the bully-boy's lips. 'And where does thou live?' he demanded.

I opened my mouth but no words fell out. What was I to say? I stared dumbly at Luke.

'Greenfield,' he shouted. 'Greenfield.'

The bully-boy swung around and pointed his sabre at Luke. 'If thou speaks again, I will rive thee through,' he bellowed. Then he turned back to me.

'Where is Greenfield?' he asked.

'Why,' I said. 'It is over there,' and I gave a wild swing of my hand that covered half the compass.

'Tell me about Greenfield.' I was ordered.

'It is, it is a village. I live there with my Dad. We are weavers and—'

As I spoke the bully-boy's smirk turned into a triumphant leer, and I must confess, although he was drunk, he had sharp ears.

'Thou art never from round here,' he cried. 'Thou art from Bolton way. We don't talk like you do round here.'

And that was that. We were hauled off down the street, and that none too gently, but before we were taken away I looked at the carter.

'You dog,' I cried. 'Why did you betray us?'

The carter gave me an impassive look, then he took the pipe from his mouth. 'You wanted to go to Mossley didn't you?' he said. 'Well, this is Mossley. What do you expect for three shillings?'

CHAPTER SIXTEEN

The Yeomen marched us through the street of Mossley as proudly as if they had captured Sir Guy Fawkes and his men and clapped us in the village pound. This was already inhabited by a stray cow which mooed when we entered, as if to say, 'Welcome'. The gate slammed behind us and the bully-boy leered at us through the bars.

'Tha'll be hunged tomorrow,' he told us. 'Us'll stretch thee from a tree!'

Luke ignored this foolish remark. 'Will you not give us food and drink?' he asked.

'Ah'll give thee a belt on the ear-hole, more like,' the Yeoman said, and lurched off, expecting no doubt to be made a general for his deeds.

I sat down and placed my face against the cool wall, feeling half ready to start skriking. Luke came over and squatted next to me. 'Never mind his foolish gabble,' he said. 'Why tomorrow . . . '

But I never did find out what Luke thought the morrow might bring, for before he had finished his sentence I had fallen into a deep and dreamless sleep.

I was awakened by the mooing of the cow. My eyes were so gummed with sleep that I had to poke at them to get them to open wide, my legs were stiff with cold, and my mouth was so parched that it was as dry as a bone. It was not quite dark. A sickly grey light was creeping through the bars and I could just make out the cow, and Luke crouching beside it. He saw my movement and came over to me.

'Here,' he said. 'Drink this—quick now.'

He grabbed my hair and pushed my head down into a sort of bag, and I found my nose stuck into a warm liquid. I stuck out my tongue and found that it was milk, cupped, as it were, in Luke's coat.

'I milked the cow,' Luke said. 'The brutes here could not be bothered.' I lapped, greedily, until I found myself licking Luke's coat, when I stopped.

'Well,' said Luke. 'Now we shall be charged with theft as well as rebellion.'

He sauntered over to the door and began running his hand over it. Although I was wonderfully refreshed by the milk, I lay inert, wondering idly what he was doing. After a while he gave over and came to me.

'I had hoped there might be a way out,' he said. 'But we might as well be in a dungeon. The lock on that door would keep a giant fast.'

As he spoke something stirred in my mind. It says something, though, for my torpor that ten or fifteen minutes had passed before I roused myself. 'A lock!' I thought. 'Why, what is a lock but a piece of machinery? And I am a mechanic. I will see this lock.' I went to the door and peered at the lock. As Luke had said, it was a massive affair of rusty iron, but old and therefore probably simple in make.

I asked Luke for a buckle off his shoe. He immediately wrenched it off and gave it me without question. I got him to hold it lengthways and crushed it under my clog, until I had a single slab of metal. This I jammed into a crack in the masonry and bent until I had an L-shape. I poked this in the lock and fumbled about for a moment, not more, for, as I had guessed, the lock being ancient had only one ward to hold it. This clicked back obligingly and the door swung open!

Luke gave me a thoughtful look but wasted no time on congratulations. He pulled his coat on, while, to avoid noise, I took off my clogs. Then we slipped away and within ten minutes were free of Mossley and heading for the high moors.

Our way ran through a maze of country lanes, but Luke seemed to know them all and before the true dawn we were on a range of black hills, well away from human habitation. There we found a stream, washed and drank, and lay down to rest for a while. I had a chance, now, to weigh up Luke. The previous day I had been aware of little more than a hand on my arm, a blue-clad back, and a cool voice; now I saw he was a weaver to the life, pale-faced and lightly built, with mild eyes, a little short-sighted. He had, too, a cool easy manner, as if to say that the world was his friend, if it could but be made to see it.

He pointed down the valley to Mossley. 'Those red-faced loons will have redder faces this morning,' he said, and grinned at the thought. Then he gave me a sideways glance. 'You did well at that lock, lad. Have you had much practice at that?'

He spoke lightly but it was plain to me what lay behind the question. I assured him that I was not a burglar but a peaceful engineer. Further, I told him what my name was and why I was in his care. At that he nodded, quite satisfied.

'I know your father, Daniel,' he said, 'and we must see that you are brought together. If any man could have brought him safe from the field, it is John.'

I was eased in my mind by this, but felt alarmed at lying on the hillside. Luke, however, bid me relax.

'We are safe enough on the moors. The Yeoman will not bring their nags up here. No, we shall take our ease for a while and then . . . well, we shall see.'

We rested longer than I would have wished, for the sun was high when we began our journey. Luke, though, was unconcerned. As we tramped through the wild heather, he whistled country tunes and several times laughed, as at some secret joke. To me he said little, save to point out the village of Oldham and its mills which lay below us on our left, and, later in the day, Rochdale. But by then I needed no guide, for beyond us lay the vale of Rossendale.

Here, in a deep cleft, we stopped at last. A brook slid gently over stone slabs, and a grove of mountain ash rustled its leaves.

'Stay here now,' said Luke, 'for I must leave you for a while. You will be safe from prying eyes but if anyone should happen past, hide yourself among the bushes. If you should be discovered, say that you are a shepherd-lad playing truant from your work. I do not like to leave you, but it must be done. I shall be back as soon as I can.' He began to move away, but then turned back. 'Daniel,' he said, seriously. 'If so be you are taken, then you must keep mum. You will do that?'

I assured him that I would, and he went away over the skyline, leaving me alone. I lay by the bank feeling tired and hungry, for I had not eaten for a day and a half. I was desperately anxious for my father, and desperately sorry for myself; and so I lay, a poor kind of wretch, until the shadows began to gather in the hollows of the moor, and in the mosses the curlews began to call. Their sad, eerie cries made the moor seem vaster, and myself smaller and lonelier, until I fancied myself merely a speck on the endless wasteland, my actions of no more consequence than those of an ant, and all the works of men mere vanity.

CHAPTER SEVENTEEN

I was roused by Luke's voice calling my name softly. He came through the grove and asked me if I had seen anyone. I told him, no, and he then bid me follow him. It was full dusk when we began to walk and by the time we had wended over the moor, we were walking in star-shine. Luke encouraged me, saying it would not be far, but it seemed a weary way to me until, at last, we came down into a deep clough, crossed a brook, and came to a cottage. Luke knocked on the door and I recognised the signal: three times quick, twice slow, and again three times quick. It was the signal of the Black Lamp!

The door opened and we entered. I was aware of the glow of a fire, a fine smell of roast mutton, and the shapes of men. One of these I recognised. That huge bulk could only be Brother John. Luke led me to the table and I was given meat and ale. The ale I drank thirstily, but as I drank I was looking for my father. John must have seen this for he sat by me and held my arm. I could see his face clearly in the light of the fire. He had a terrible gash over his forehead and his eyes and nose were as black as soot. He caught my gaze and gave a rueful grin.

'Some of us are born to trouble, hey?' Then he gave me a friendly blow on the shoulder. 'At least I am alive to tell the tale,' he paused and grinned again. 'And so is your father, although I dare say his head is as sore as mine.'

He gave me a hearty grin but I was too much a-tremble to give him one back, indeed my hand shook so much that I spilled some ale from my mug. 'Where is he now?' I cried, and rose, ready to be off there and then.

'Easy, lad,' John said. 'Easy now. He is a good step from here. I took him from under the noses of the Cavalry and he is lying in Stockport. He is safe enough there, and he is being cared for. He was cut bad by Cranley, and ridden over too. But I daresay he will live and he must lie low anyway. The troopers are rounding up all who were leaders in the march, and be sure his name is on the list.'

'Well I must go there,' I said. 'And when he is well bring him back home. I will wait until it is dark and find my way over the moors.'

John gave me a heavy look. 'I think it best if you do not do that,' he said. 'Believe me, he is in good hands—and he knows that you are safe. Best for you to wait here.'

'But what about my sister?' I cried. 'If I cannot go to Stockport, then I had best get off home. She will be frightened with her father and me away.'

'You have a sister?' It was Luke who spoke and as he did so the good humour faded from his eyes.

'Why, yes,' I answered.

'And how old is she?'

'Ten.'

'And is she being looked after?'

'Yes, a woman is caring for her. One of my father's friends.'

'Well,' Luke said. 'We must rest thankful for that.' He came from his seat by the fire and joined us at the table. There was a certain diffident awkwardness in his manner, and although I was young, I was old enough to see that what was to come would not be pleasant, and my instinct proved right.

Luke tapped the table thoughtfully. 'I know that it is hard for you to think of your father wounded and among men strange to you, and it is hard for you to think of your sister, lonely and frightened, but it is not possible for you to leave just now.'

'Why not?' I demanded. 'My house is just over the valley. I can find my way there blindfolded.'

Luke shook his head. 'The countryside is swarming with troops and constables. There will be a watch on every village, be sure of that.'

I let this sink in for a moment and then opened my mouth to speak again, but I was interrupted by the other men, who had risen and were collecting their possessions. I could hardly see their faces, and their voices were not much more revealing, for they merely made a few gruff farewells and slouched out into the night. Seeing them going made me thoughtful.

'I will be off, too,' I announced, and stood up.

Luke and John glanced at each other and then Luke turned his face to me and smiled. 'Now then,' he said. 'I thought that I had made clear why it will be best for you to stay here, Daniel.'

I admitted that. 'But they have gone, those men. Why should I stay?'

'They are men, Daniel, and, when all is said and done, you are only a lad. If they are picked up they are well able to hold their tongues, but should you be taken a magistrate might easily trip you up and get from you that which might imperil us all. I think that you will see my point there.'

'I will not speak if I am caught,' I said, hotly.

'You may not think so,' Luke said, 'but, do you see, our necks are in your hands. You would not like to place your life in the hands of a lad, would you?'

I could hardly say no to that but I was too young to say so. I stared stubbornly at the table-top, behaviour which must have confirmed the two men in their judgement that I was not the lad to trust with their lives.

'Will you not agree to stay?' Luke urged. When I refused to answer him he turned to John with a helpless shrug. John growled deep in his throat and some of the joviality went from his battered face.

'I have spoken to your father,' he said, 'before all this, when we were getting the Hampden Clubs together. He told me something of this Cranley. It seems that he was a spy in the old days. Cranley suspects that your father knows that, and he might well believe that you know it too, you and your Dad being so close. As it is, for all Cranley knows, your father might be dead. In which case you could be the only one left who knows his secret. It would be a powerful argument for him to deal with you as he did with your father—cut you down like a heifer.'

There was sense in that, too, but still I would not see it and stared sulkily at the fire. John, with more patience than I would have thought him capable of, tried again.

'Do you not understand me? And besides, you know the names of many of us who have called at your house. If they were got from you, then we would be charged with conspiracy and our past would come out—why, they would have the rope ready before the jury was sworn in. You must stay, lad, you must.'

I could not deny the sense of this but the more I was talked at, the more stubborn I became and when John had finished I rose to my feet.

'You may say what you wish, but I have a sister who will be crying for me now.'

'Then I am sorry,' said Luke. He did not move, nor did John, but I felt a change in their manner. John's eyes grew dark, and the friendly wrinkles around Luke's eyes crinkled into more sinister lines. I hovered uncertainly for a moment then took a step towards the door, but before I had gone further John had me by the arm, and his grip was like a vice.

Luke regarded us both and spoke again. His voice was as light as usual, but the banter had gone from it.

'I think that you will be staying for a while, Dan,' he said.

I was flabbergasted at this. 'Do you mean that I am prisoner?' I asked.

'I suppose that describes it,' Luke said. 'Although we are unwilling gaolers. You will be free to go in a day or so, but stay you must.' Saying this he opened a door which led into a small room. 'We will make you as comfortable as can be. In!'

I shrugged angrily under John's grasp. 'I will not go in there,' I said.

'Come now,' Luke said. 'Stay you must and it will be best to stay in here. Then you will have no temptation to run away.'

He pointed firmly to the door. There was no point in resisting John so I walked forward reluctantly and found myself in a poky room, with a small window high in the wall.

'Settle down, Daniel,' said Luke. 'There is a bed for you.'

I glanced at the window. Luke saw me do this and smiled. 'There are stout shutters for that—and the door has a bar, on our side. I am afraid that there will be no call for your mechanical skills tonight.'

With that he closed the door on me. I will not tire you with my feelings when I heard the door slam. For the second time in three days I was a prisoner, and now my gaolers were those I had believed were my friends. In a rage I hammered at the door but had the sense, at last, to give up such futility. I threw myself on the bed. Through the window I could see the stars shining but they were soon obliterated as a shutter was slammed to. And so I lay in the dark, scarce able to keep my tears away, until sleep came and took all from me.

I was kept in the room for three days. At first I spent a deal of time with my ear against the door. There was much coming and going: footsteps, the murmur of conversation, John's rough voice. But I heard nothing of sense or meaning. The weather broke, there was a steady drizzle, and I could hear the brook splash and gurgle outside my gaol. I took to lying on the bed for hours, listening to it, counting the stones on the walls, and the spiders which ran across them. I was well fed and was allowed out once or twice a day to wash and relieve myself, always under guard. Then the cottage fell silent. There was no longer the clatter and rattle of men moving and talking. I thought that I had been deserted and fell into a terrible panic, thinking that I had been left to starve to death, but I heard Luke's voice singing, and fell back into my torpor.

Then, one evening, the door opened and Luke stood in the doorway with his coat on and a stick in his hand. 'Come, Daniel,' he said. 'The days of thy Babylonish captivity are over.'

I rose from the bed and went through the door. 'Here is your coat, Daniel,' Luke said.

I took it from him and put it on. 'Am I free to go now?' I asked coldly.

'Yes,' said Luke. 'But I thought we might go together.'

'No,' I cried. 'I will go by myself.' And I made for the door.

Luke moved over sharply. 'Listen, lad. You do not want to go on your own. It will be best if we go together. You are sullen now because you have not had your own way. I understand that. It was no pleasure to lock you up but the others had to have their chance to go free, and it had to be a fair one. John, now: he waited here to aid others when he could have got off, taking his life in his hands by doing so. Now he is on a ship to America, and the others who can are away. It would not have been just to place their lives in the hands of a boy.' He held out his hand appealingly. 'You are a lad of sense and will see the justice of that.'

No sensible man would have resisted that outstretched hand, but it was easy for a sulky boy and so I looked away. Luke stared at me thoughtfully for a moment.

'Will you sit for a moment?' he asked, and when I stayed where I was, glaring stubbornly at the floor, he touched my arm. 'What I have to say is important. It concerns your father.'

That I could not resist. I sat on the edge of a rough stool. 'Well?'

'A man came, while you were in there.' Luke nodded at the room. 'He said that your father is alive still, although he is badly hurt. He is not in Stockport, though. The magistrates were searching all the houses there for Radicals and so he has been taken to Spen Valley, to be cared for there. It will be a long time before he can move freely, or work, but he has many friends in Spen and they will care for him.'

I did not show much emotion at this news. I rather hugged it to myself, letting my gladness warm my heart. So undisturbed did I seem that Luke peered closely at me. 'You understand what I am saying?' he asked.

I gave a nod, but was still lout enough not to thank Luke for his words. Another man would have clouted my lug there and then, but he merely smiled a little. 'Have you nothing to say?' he asked.

'Well,' I mumbled, somewhat red-faced and shy. 'I am glad to hear it.'

'And do you not see what follows from that? If your father is in Spen—where will you go?'

I frowned at Luke for at first I did not catch his drift. In my mind I still believed that in the hour I would be in my home at Helmshaw, playing with Emma before the fire as my father worked at the loom, and that I would, soon enough, be lying down in my own bed with nothing more to concern me than rising on the morrow to go to my work.

'Do you have any plans?' Luke asked again.

I gave him a stupid, vacant stare. 'Plans?' I repeated, and then it occurred to me that my mind was empty. I had no plans, nor any ideas of plans. I had a wounded father in Spen, a child to care for, I was jobless and had a vindictive enemy in Cranley—that I was aware of, or was becoming aware of—but how to deal with these things, of that I had no more idea than the man in the moon. I groped at the first thing that came into my head. 'Why is my father in Spen?'

Luke hesitated, a little exasperated by the question I thought, but he answered. 'I have told you that, your father has many friends in the Valley.' He paused again then banged the table firmly. 'Daniel, has your father ever told you of the Black Lamp?'

I said that he had. 'But it was long ago when he was in it.'

'That it was,' Luke said. 'It seems like a hundred years off; but it is not forgotten in Spen, nor are those who led it. Spen was its stronghold in Yorkshire. I doubt if there was one man there who did not know of it. You know John was a leader? And your father? Well I was one too. We swore an oath—and we could have been hanged for that—an oath to eternal friendship. That oath took John back onto St. Peter's field to save your father, it is that which has taken your father from under the noses of the magistrates, and it is that oath which binds me to you. Now we must look to the future. You cannot stay in your village. This Cranley will hound you down, be sure of that. And besides, how will you earn your living? Now if you are willing it may be wise for you to come with me. I am going home to Spen and we can get your sister and the three of us slip over the moors. I have a wife there who will care for her and it may be that we can find you work as a mechanic. If not then you can turn to at the loom with me. You will be near your father and you all three will be safe. No one in Spen will run to the magistrates, not that I am saying they would here. At any rate, it is more sensible than anything else I can think of. How does that sound to you?'

The truth was that it sounded very good sense, and more than that. It was like a deliverance. I felt that I had dipped my toe into the waters of maturity—and found them too cold for me. But still I was too stupid to admit this.

Luke waited for a while and then rose. 'Well,' he said. 'I shall walk with you to your village. It is on my way, and if we are to be arrested I should be glad to have you with me, hey?'

I made no answer to this but I did not object either, and so we set off together. It was full dark now and there was a steady drizzle, but there was a moon and we made our way down the brook without difficulty and followed a footpath which snaked towards the pike, which shone like silver in the moonlight. We went cautiously, keeping our ears pricked, but the night was as quiet as the grave. We nipped over the pike and slid into the fields on the other side. After a while Luke halted.

'Now lad,' he said. 'I am in your hands. You must make the decisions and lead the way. I will follow.'

This pleased me greatly. I, who had been for so long at the disposal of others, was now the responsible man. Having the responsibility made me stand a little straighter and walk a little firmer. It also made me think more sensibly and I began to see the generosity of Luke's offer, and the good reasoning behind it. I also reflected on the decency of men who would risk their necks for an oath sworn twenty years ago, and when we paused by the Irwell, which rushed past us, smooth with the rains of the past few days, I told him so.

He made no fuss over this but patted my shoulder, and when we started off again I, for one, walked with a lighter step. There was no chance of crossing the river by any ford and so I made upstream to the bridge at Chadderton. There were scattered cottages there so we went with caution. But even so the dogs caught wind of us and howled, one to the other, until it seemed as if every dog in England was howling, 'Traitors here, Radicals!' In my new-found adulthood I thought it fitting to mutter an oath at the dogs, as bad a one as I could muster, but I was taken aback when Luke gave me a sharp poke in the ribs and told me to save such language for the likes of Cranley.

We made it across the bridge and up through Snig Hole, crept past Fenner's Clough, and, as the church clock in Haslingden was striking the hour, we padded up Helmshaw moor and came to our house.

CHAPTER EIGHTEEN

It says something for my innocence when I tell you that despite all that had happened, and despite all that I had been told, I fully expected to see a light shining through the window and to hear the clacking of the loom. But the house was deserted and as dark as the grave. I stared at it for a minute and turned to Luke.

'There is no one here,' I said.

'No,' Luke spoke gently but without surprise. 'Maybe we had best try the people who are looking after your sister. What name did you say they had?'

I did not recall telling him but I murmured it. 'Adshead.'

'Adshead,' Luke repeated. 'What manner of man might he be?'

I described James and said that he and father had been good friends.

'That should be good enough,' said Luke. 'Well, lead the way.'

We slipped down the backs of the gardens until we came to the path which led to James' house. I would have sauntered up and banged on the door but Luke held me back.

He went up the path, scraped up some small stones, and chucked them at the window over the door. After a minute or two the window opened and James' voice demanded to know who was disturbing him.

'A friend from Manchester,' Luke whispered. 'Have you any troops quartered on you?'

'No, that I have not,' said James. 'And I have no friends in Manchester either.'

At that Luke drew me forward under the window so that James could see me.

'Wait there,' James said. A moment later the door opened and we hastened inside. James seized me, his face as white as a sheet.

'Thank God you are safe,' he cried, but he was looking over my shoulder at Luke.

'Do I know you, friend?' he asked.

'Maybe, maybe not,' answered Luke. 'But I know you.'

'I think not,' said James. 'But you have a strange way of waking folk.'

Luke smiled. 'I learned that a long time ago.' Then he leaned forward and whispered in James' ear. What it was I did not catch, but James shook when he heard it.

'Do not say those words,' he cried. The candle in his hand trembled as he spoke and shadows flickered across our faces. They seemed to me like ghosts jumping from the past and I remembered that night, years ago, when John and Bamford had come from the darkness as we had done this night, knocking strange knocks and whispering stranger words. I thought of the fears I had then—and how those fears had come true.

For a moment the three of us were as still as statues, then Mrs. Adshead burst into the room.

'Oh Daniel,' she cried, and clamped my head under her arm with a grip like a prize-fighter. 'Oh lad, I thought the dragons had thee. Where is thy father?'

'Aye, where is he?' asked James.

We told him of father's state and something of our adventures. Mrs. Adshead burst into tears and rushed into the scullery where she rattled plates, a sound I listened to hopefully. My thought was not only on my belly, though I cast a glance up the stairs, thinking of Emma sleeping there and, despite all, believing that our troubles were coming to an end. I opened my mouth to speak of her but James was talking in a fast, excited gabble.

'I lost sight of you when the horse-soldiers charged. Thomas Spencer was cut very bad. I tried to get him away but the constables took him. He is in the New Bailey now. Sam Teller was trampled on but he got home. All the Saints were scattered and Briggs' wife was killed. Briggs has gone mad. He roams the moors like a wolf, howling and shrieking. He tried to burn the mill down and kill Cranley but the soldiers drove him off. Cranley has soldiers in the mill . . .'

He gabbled on looking wretched and fidgety. Mrs. Adshead came in with bread and cheese and looked at us tearfully but still James chattered. At last I broke in.

'And Emma, how is she?'

'Emma?' James repeated in a vacant way.

'Why yes, is she well or ill?'

James shook his head. 'I cannot tell.'

I felt a sick apprehension. 'Why not, why cannot you tell?'

'Because she is not here.'

I could not believe that I had heard aright. 'But she must be here.'

'No. Cranley has her.'

I stared hopelessly at James.

'It is true,' he said. 'Cranley came the day after the March and said that the Parish had 'prenticed her to the mill. He had two constables with him. There was nothing we could do.'

James looked as distraught as I felt and we might well have had an old wives' sobbing match but for Luke.

'We must get the child back,' he said firmly.

'You must,' cried Mrs. Adshead. 'When I think of that poor child there—' Her eyes flooded with tears again but she mastered them. 'You must go to the Parish, Daniel, and tell them to return her.'

Luke shook his head. 'We cannot do that. If Daniel shows his face then he will be taken by the constables for sure. It may be that is the reason Cranley has done such a vile thing, that he may draw Daniel to him. Remember Daniel knows secrets of Cranley's past.'

'Well then,' said James. 'Our position is hopeless, for not a mouse can get in the mill. It is guarded as closely as a fortress.'

'I have seen fortresses fall before.' Luke spoke as calmly as though he was a master of sappers and took one every week. 'This lad and I were locked in one not a week ago but it failed to hold us for three hours. Come now, Daniel, how can we get Emma out?'

I was as doleful as James. 'We would have to find her first. She could be anywhere: in the spinning room, or the children's dormitory, or the felting shed, or in Burns' rooms, or in Cranley's house . . .' I could not bring myself to continue and my voice flagged.

We fell silent then. James and Mrs. Adshead and myself stared gloomily at the fire, but Luke did not lose his composure.

'That is a good point. Is there someone in the mill who might help us? A weaver, like, who has been driven to work there?'

James was firm. 'We have no friends in the mill.'

'But we have,' I cried. 'There is Bloom!'

'Who is he?' Luke asked.

I told him but he was not impressed. 'He is an engineer. He will be no friend to the weavers. His like are driving us into the gutter.'

'Maybe,' I answered. 'But Bloom has always been a friend to me. And anyway, I am an engineer myself.'

Luke gave me a sharp glance when I said that. 'So you are, Daniel. I had forgotten that. Well, if this man will hold his tongue there is no harm in asking him. It is a chancy business but we must take a chance now and then in this world or we would never move. How can we get hold of this Bloom?'

I told him and said that I was ready to go and see him there and then, for it was plain that the quicker we did what we had to do the better. But Luke gave the no to this.

'I will go. It is best all round if you are not seen in these parts. Where does this man live?'

We told him where to find Bloom, whose house was only a cock-stride away, and he sauntered to the door. 'I will see you later,' he said casually.

'And if we don't?' James asked.

'Well,' Luke hesitated for a moment. 'Well, in that case forget me friends. But you might remember that I have a wife in Spen. Anyone there knows me. The Professor they call me. Because of my bad eyes, I suppose.'

With that he was away. We waited an uneasy half-hour, fidgeting about, talking half-heartedly of the village and its doings until we heard a triple knock at the door. When James opened it, in walked Luke and Bloom.

I was astonished, in a way, to see Bloom at all. It was as if he was from some previous existence, a half-remembered figure from childhood instead of the familiar yellow shape with whom

I had worked not many days before. He came and sat by the door, ran his hands over his long face, and gave a doleful sigh.

'So you are here, Daniel,' he said, as if there might be some doubt in his mind about it. 'Well, you need my help I hear.'

'Yes, for Emma, do you see.'

'I see it all right,' said Bloom. 'I can see it well enough. But it is one thing to see and another to do. However, what I can do I will. Your politics are none of my affair but I will help for the child's sake.'

'Well said!' Luke banged the table. 'Now, how best can we go about it?'

Bloom shrugged. 'Your guess is as good as mine there, but I will tell you this. You must do it quick for Cranley is sending her to Fletcher's mill in Bury on Sunday, and it's Friday today.'

My jaw dropped at that. I goggled at Bloom. 'Sunday!' I cried.

'That is so. I heard him telling Burns this very day. He wants the girl in secure hands, away from the weavers of this village.'

James waved his arms feebly, as if to say, 'What is to be done?' and I was not more lively. To get Emma from the mill was one thing, to get her out in the short space of time that remained to us was another. It was a problem which I could not answer. It was Luke who prodded us again.

'Do you have a free hand in the mill?' he asked Bloom.

'More or less. I spend a lot of time in the new mill putting in the fire-engines. Fine engines they are, too. The boring on the cylinders is so smooth . . .'

I saw his eyes begin to glitter and could not resist a smile. Bloom saw it and tilted his head sheepishly.

'Well . . .' he said.

Luke gazed at Bloom wonderingly but kept to the point. 'You can get in this other mill though?' he asked in a tone of voice which meant that there was to be no further talk of the boring of cylinders, no matter how fine it might be.

'Oh yes, any time I like.'

'And where is the lass kept?'

'In the dormitory with the other children. There is no need for special treatment. The whole place is like a prison.'

'And what is the dormitory like?'

Bloom looked surprised. 'Why, I do not know. It has nothing to do with me.'

Luke frowned and turned to me. 'What is it like Daniel?'

I, too, had to confess ignorance. 'I have never been in there.'

'You have been in the mill for five years and never seen how the children are kept?' Luke sounded incredulous and angry too. But before we had time to offer a defence he had moved on.

'What is the mill like? How can we best go about this business?'

I was somewhat diffident for I had been shaken by Luke's anger about my ignorance of the dormitory, but I answered.

'There is a wall around the mill. I could climb that but I doubt that Emma could. There are big gates at the front of the mill for the waggons. They have a little wicket-gate set in them for when they don't want to open the main gates. And there is another little gate at the back of the mill, behind Cranley's house. That is all.'

Bloom shook his head. 'You can forget climbing the wall. Cranley has put spikes along it and there are soldiers walking about. You will have to come in through the gate, if you get in at all.'

'To do that the gate must be opened.' Luke tapped the table, his eyes on Bloom.

'I know that, man.' Bloom said. 'And I will see that the wicket gate is open and I will try and distract the guard. Then you must come in and take the child if you can. It is a risky business though, and if Cranley or Burns is about then I will have to leave it.'

'I understand,' said Luke. 'We will have to think again if that is the case.' He paused and coughed. 'You would not care to fetch the child out would you? It would make matters easier.'

Bloom's face hardened. 'No, I would not care to bring her out. What I am going to do is risky enough, but if I were caught with the child it would be theft and I would find a rope around my neck. If what I have offered to do is not enough, then say so.'

'Not at all, not at all.' Luke was soothing, anxious not to offend nor lose an ally. 'I asked too much of you.'

Bloom was not so easily mollified. 'I am going to open the gate, why don't you come in and get her?'

'Why, I would do that,' Luke said. 'But I am a stranger to the child. It would frighten her to death if I appeared in the middle of the night and seized her. It needs must be one whom the child knows, and better if it is one who knows his way about the mill.'

I looked around at the men. What Luke had said was common sense, any fool could see that. But Bloom was sulky and obdurate and James was white with terror, lest he be asked. But there was no need for him to fear. Although I might often have rued it, I had cared for Emma since she had first left her cradle. She was my charge, doubly so now that father was away. Taking her from Cranley's dirty grasp was no man's task but mine. And, indeed, that night, truly, I became a man.

'I will go,' I said. 'Who else?'

Luke gazed at me steadily through his pale blue eyes. 'Aye,' he said. 'Who else?'

He paused for a moment, as if giving Bloom and James a chance to speak, but both remained silent.

'Very well, then. Bloom here will try and open the gate and Daniel will slip in and try and get the child. I would go in with him but it seems to me that the fewer of us there are creeping about in there the better. But I will wait by the mill in case there is anything I can do. Now, we must cover our retreat, as the generals say. Suppose that he gets the girl. How does he come out? Remember, the gate might be guarded by then. Bloom here might not be able to keep the guard away for ever.'

'That I can't,' Bloom cried. 'I will have to get off the mill or Cranley will start to wondering what's up.'

I had kept pretty quiet until then but I thought that it was time I had my say, especially as it was I who was going to go into the mill.

'I can always try the gate at the back; but if that can't be done then I can take a rope with me and maybe climb up the wall where it is dark, by the tenter-sheds perhaps. If I had a rope then I could pull Emma up. I will have to cope with the spikes somehow.'

Bloom gave a sour grunt. 'It sounds all right, but where's the rope?'

James stood up then. 'Why, look about you.'

He waved his hand and we stared at the hanks of woollen yarn which hung from the rafters. 'If we cannot make a rope from all that then we are no weavers.'

For a moment we all contemplated the slender hanks, dangling and swaying in the draughts, then Bloom rose.

'I'm off,' he said. 'It sounds a daft scheme to me, but I always said that you lot up here weren't right in the head. I'll open the gate tomorrow night when the mill has shut down. It should be about ten o'clock.'

Luke nodded his assent to this but Mrs. Adshead had something to say.

'How will the lad know that it is safe to go into the mill? The gate might be open but have a soldier standing with his back to it. He must have a signal that all is well.'

'Right enough Missus,' Bloom agreed. He screwed up his face as if he had the toothache, but, in fact, in thought. Then he slapped his thigh.

'I have it. If all is well then I will jam a piece of wool in the wicket. If anyone else should see it they will not be suspicious, but if Daniel sees it he will know that all's clear.'

He looked around with a pleased air. Luke sprang to his feet and clapped him on the shoulder crying, 'Well done!' I believe that he was anxious to please Bloom after their coldness earlier.

Bloom accepted the congratulations then made for the door. 'I'll be off, then. You take care, Daniel. If you are taken then there is nothing I can do for you. And my name must not be mentioned.'

We thanked him and promised that his name would never be revealed. James blew out the candle and Mrs. Adshead shielded the fire with her shawl. Bloom opened the door a crack and peered through. All was quiet enough and Bloom made to go out. But as he did so there came a scream from the darkness. It was a hideous wail that sounded as if it came from nothing human. But then it became so full of unendurable distress and agony that only something human could have uttered it.

Luke started back. 'What the devil's that?'

James closed the door on the sound. 'It is Briggs. I told you he wanders the moors.'

'Why does he scream so?' Luke's voice was troubled and had its own distress.

'Why? He cries for the loss of his wife and home. He cries for the loss of his hopes and beliefs. He expected to see an angel with a fiery sword come and cut down his enemies, but 'twas he was cut down. Why should he not cry—or any of us?'

James' grim reply silenced us. There was little further talk as we set to making our rope. But as we worked I could not but think of the Black Lamp and its oath, and how, as the many single threads we wove would make one strong rope, so many individuals were to have made one strong army. But the Lamp had failed—the weavers starved while the machines clacked; the Great March had failed—we were hunted fugitives and Cranley worked his mill as if our efforts had never taken place. I wondered whether every attempt of the poor men was bound to fail—and Briggs' cry seemed to ring in my ears saying, 'It would, it would'.

By an hour after sunrise we had finished the rope. James tied a loop in it and threw it over a beam. He swung on it and it took his weight easily.

'It seems stout enough,' he said.

It did. It looked stout enough to hang a man, and I do not think that thought was far from any of our minds as we watched it swing to and fro, to and fro.

CHAPTER NINETEEN

With the rope made there was nothing for it but to wait, and a long wait it seemed. Of necessity we had to stay indoors and dared not so much as peep through the window. I cat-napped on and off but was mighty glad when night came and Luke, James, and I, with the rope round my shoulders, could leave the house.

Our final plan was that the three of us should go down to the mill. If I got in, Luke was going to wait nearby, ready to help when I got out, if I got out. But as we three went through the dark fields I felt brave and confident. It seemed a small thing to go into the mill and take my sister from under Cranley's nose. I was so brave that I was impatient of James' caution, for he hugged every shadow as we went along. Near the mill we paused in a copse. Luke took my arm.

'You are ready?' he asked.

I whispered that I was, but my mouth was dry with excitement and I could hardly get the words out. Luke was quick to catch the hoarseness in my speech.

'Are you afraid?' he asked. 'Do you wish me to go?'

I was huffed at the suggestion that I should be thought capable of such a human emotion as fear and shrugged his arm off impatiently. Luke wasted no further time on me but slapped my back. James gave me a muffled good-bye, and, without further ado, I made off.

It was no more than a couple of hundred yards to the mill but it took me an interminable time to get there for I crawled on my stomach through the wet grass. As I edged closer I found that I was growing distinctly less brave until, by the time I had reached the mill-wall, all my vain-glory had quite gone. I found then that I did not, after all, wish to creep about Cranley's mill seeking my sister. What I really wanted to do was to sit by a fireside, drinking tea and listening to ghost stories. I hoped, very deeply, that Bloom would not have been able to carry out his promise and open the wicket-gate. Nourishing this hope I sidled along the mill-wall and looked at the gates. A hank of wool hung from them.

I looked at the wool for a long time. I believe that I touched it for I have a distinct recollection that it was damp from the evening dew. I remember, too, that I took a step backwards, as from some dreadful sight. Above me the mill loomed: black, blank, forbidding, blotting out the stars. It looked as though immortality had been built into every stone. I cannot tell how small and weak I felt looking at it. I thought with some bitterness how, but a week before, I had marched with a host I thought invincible, banners had floated over my head, drums and trumpets had lightened my heart and quickened my step. Now I was creeping about the mill on my belly like a rat.

I nearly took to my heels then; but yet . . . the hank of wool hung from the gate. I could see it glimmer and something within me told me that if I went I would not soon forget it. It was a signal, do you see: the bastion held its own enemy, indeed had created it. Something human lived in its brute world of iron and profit. I could not walk away. To do so would have meant ceasing to be human myself. I do not say that I thought in just those terms then.

I went back to the wicket, opened it a crack, and slipped into the mill.

The yard was not quite dark. A light shone from Cranley's cottage across the yard, and another from the dormitory, which was on my right. I edged towards the dormitory and then, from the other side of the gate, I heard voices. I froze in the darkness, scarcely daring to breathe. The voices came towards me. One I recognised, it was Bloom's. At the gate the men stopped. I heard Bloom clearly.

'What's a sergeant but an officer's pet? Why, you are as good as ten sergeants, any fool can see that.'

Whoever he was talking to clearly did not disagree with this for a rough voice swore that Bloom was the sharpest man in

Lancashire. I was glad to hear Bloom. It was comforting to know that I had an ally near me. But then Bloom said good night. He had to say it several times before it was accepted. There was some fumbling with bolts and bars and, in the end, a reluctant 'farewell' from the rough voice. The gate clattered to, and then I was truly alone in the mill.

I guessed the guard had a musket for I heard the clatter of a stock on the cobbles. There was no more sound for a moment. I waited and heard an odd snorting noise. It took me a moment to realise that it was a snore!

This cheered me up no end. If the rest of the guards were as conscientious as this one I was at less risk than I had imagined. Emboldened, I sidled along the mill-wall to the dormitory, keeping in the deep shadow. There was a space between the building and the wall but I took a chance and kept on the yard side, for I wished to take a look through the window and see what Burns was up to. I did not think there was any risk of me being seen from the inside, indeed the window was so dirty that when I glanced in I could hardly see anything. But I could make out Burns sitting at a table, guzzling a mound of potatoes. His wife was sitting in a smashed-up chair with her nose stuck in a glass of gin. They made a pretty pair, more like two pigs in a sty than humans charged with the care of children. But there was something else in the room which interested me. Sprawled on a settle were two red-coats, one a corporal, each with a glass in his hand. I wished them hearty swigging and hoped they would get drunk as soon as possible.

I dropped to my knees and scuttled under the window to the entrance to the dormitory. The door was open and I could see down a passage to Burns' room. His door was half open but I did not think anyone in the room would be able to see me. The passage was gloomy and littered with odds and ends from the mill. A burst of laughter came from Burns' room and I started back, fearful that someone was coming out . . . No one appeared though, and I took a deep breath and tiptoed forward.

Although I had to go carefully among the debris I found its presence useful, for it gave me some cover as I went along. The dangerous bit was getting to the stairs, which meant crossing the light from the room. The stairs were no more than a rough wooden ladder, but stoutly made, so I did not think that I need worry about creaks. I hesitated for a moment, wondering whether to go up them quickly or slowly. In the end I half jumped across the passage and went up the steps like a squirrel. I will not deny that when I reached the top I felt a glow of triumph. Despite walls and soldiers, locks and bars, I had made my way to the dormitory. I was within a stride or two of Emma.

There were no lights in the room but it was not quite dark. I let my eyes adjust to the changed light, then took a step inside.

As far as I could make out the room was long and narrow, with a trestle table down the middle. There were no chairs. On the table were bowls. It was clear that they had not been washed, nor would they be that night, and the room stank of sour gruel. It was not the only smell. The room was so full of the fetid odours of misery that the air was more like a foul and choking blanket. As well, the thick air was full of small sounds: tiny cries, whimpers, rustles, restless sad noises, as though all the evils from Pandora's box were creeping about the room, although, to be sure, it was only the sound of the children moving in their miseries.

I called softly. 'Emma. Emma?'

Somewhere a child gave a throaty whimper and another cried out, 'Dogs!' in its sleep, but there was no answer from Emma.

For a moment I was nonplussed. I had half expected that on my calling her, Emma would come pattering to me and we would be off. I hovered uncertainly for a moment and then knelt by the mattress nearest to me. Gently I put out my hand and touched a child's head. It moved a little but made no sound. I drew back the blanket as carefully as I could. Whether it was a boy or girl in the bed I had no way of telling, for all the children's hair was hacked to the same length. It was awake and stared at me unwinkingly, showing neither fear, nor curiosity, nor any human emotion at all.

'Do you know a girl called Emma?' I asked.

The child gave no answer and I had a fearful thought that it might be dead. I touched its forehead but it was warm. Its eyes flickered when I did that. It was the only sign of life it gave. I tucked the blanket back and moved to the next crib. Again I whispered Emma's name but the small shape under the blanket lay inert, oblivious. I turned the blanket down. The child was lost in an exhausted sleep, so deep that it seemed it would not waken before the Last Trump. Its thumb was in its mouth.

I stole down the room looking at each child. Most of them were in a coma-like sleep, although I hardly like to use that word for it has a pleasant ring to it. One child who was awake and whimpering stopped instantly when I leaned over her. Another gave a high shrill cry, something like a vixen calling. From downstairs came a bellow and I heard footsteps on the stairs. Burns shouted up savagely that he had something for skriking brats, but he came no further.

By now I had gone down one row of beds. I crossed the room and searched the cribs on the other side. I peered at child after child but could not find Emma. And then I moved on to the next bed—only to find that there was none. I had searched every bed.

My heart sank. For a second I was too stupefied even to think. I stared at the floor unbelievingly, as if a bed with Emma in it would materialise there if I looked long enough. I was jerked from my trance by a shout from downstairs. I went to the head of the stairs and listened. Some sort of dirty, drunken row had broken out. After a while it quieted down and I set myself to thinking. If Emma was not in the dormitory, where could she be? It was possible that Cranley had her in his cottage or Burns in his rooms. But Bloom had been certain that she was kept with the other children. In the end I did the only thing I could do. Hoping that I had missed a bed, I went down the dormitory again.

I found Emma in the third bed down. I had not failed to look there, I simply had not recognised her when I saw her. I had been looking for a round-faced child with a confiding air, even in sleep. Instead I looked down on a wraith with a face as sharp and brittle as a vole's skull, save where a swelling disfigured her forehead.

Below, Burns and the soldiers burst into a drunken song, and Mrs. Burns gave a whooping laugh. Both the laughter and the song sounded like a blasphemy to me.

I shook Emma gently. She did not stir. I made to wake her again but left off. There seemed no point in waking her if it could be avoided. Instead I slipped my arm under her shoulder and drew her up. She, whose weight used to make me puff when I carried her any distance, came from the bed as lightly as a feather. But she was disturbed by the movement and her eyes opened.

'Emma,' I said, and gave her as good a smile as I could muster.

She stared at me and a look of terror crossed her gaunt face. She did not scream but wriggled mutely.

'Emma,' I kept my voice soft. 'It's Daniel, Daniel, your brother.'

My hope that this would soothe her was vain. She twisted her face from mine as though the Devil was looking at her and opened her mouth ready to scream. I was forced to put my hand over her mouth to smother the cry. As I did that, as I was forced to maltreat my sister, I was seized with a blind hatred of Cranley and all his works. What malignancy, I thought, could bring about such a situation where a child could look with terror on her brother. As I crushed her I had it in mind that I would come back to the mill and kill Burns and Cranley.

Emma gave another convulsive jerk.

'Do you not understand?' I whispered. 'It's Daniel. I have come to fetch you home.'

She did not answer me. Her eyes, dark and shadowed, were fixed on my face. I have seen such a look on a trapped and wounded animal. Thinking an everyday term might calm her I asked her where her clothes were. She did not answer, and indeed it was unnecessary, for she was fully clad. In Cranley's mill, it seemed, there was no need for the children to undress when they went to bed.

There seemed little use in saying more. I forced her face against my shoulder and went to the stairs. As I went, some of the children turned their heads and watched me. It was hard not to think of those who were to be left behind. Emma and I might get free but what was left for them in life? At best a few more years of dull fatigue, the slow paralysis of starvation, and then extinction. I wondered what was in their minds, seeing a man creep about in the darkness and take out a child. The worst thought I had that night was that they might not think it strange.

I waited again at the head of the stairs, and wisely. Within a minute the soldiers lurched out of Burns' room and banged their way out into the yard. After a minute or two Burns' light went out. I gave him a while longer to settle in, then cautiously made my way downstairs. It was no easy matter in the dark, and with Emma in my arms, but I got down all right, and down the passage too. The door had been left open so that I was saved any fumbling with locks and, without fuss, I found myself in the mill-yard.

To give myself time to see how things were I fell back into the shadow of the wall. It was as well I did. Two soldiers came marching across the yard in as military a way as anyone could wish for. I was bitterly disappointed for I had hoped that the garrison would be in a drunken slumber. It was clear, now, that I would not be able to get back through the gate and must try another way. After a moment's hesitation I got rid of the rope. I did not think that Emma was in any state to climb a wall. That left only one way, the gate behind Cranley's house.

The way there led me past the spinning shed. Like the dormitory there was a gap between it and the wall where the tenter-sheds were. I went down there, past the ghostly sheets of cloth, and came out under the arc of the water-wheel. All was still. The only sounds were the water gurgling in the lodge and an owl hooting beyond the wall. Emma was still silent but some of the rigidity had gone from her body. I took a look at her face.

Her eyes were still open but I managed to console myself into thinking that some of the glassy terror had gone.

From where we stood I could see Cranley's house. It was but a few yards away. I covered the distance in a darting rush and within a few paces we were crouching in a corner, against the wall and the fence which blocked off Cranley's yard. It was maddening to think that there was only the thickness of a few stones between us and freedom.

The fence was a little higher than I, about five feet six, and made of rough boarding. I peered through a chink in the wood. A light was on in the cottage and I could see into its bleak interior. The clerk was scratching away at a desk and Cranley himself was standing under the lamp, looking closely at a piece of cloth. The light came down the yard, but not very far: the wall, and the gate, were in darkness. I wondered whether to wait longer. Although the gate was in darkness there was risk in trying for it with the men not ten yards away. But Cranley could be up half the night, and someone might take it into his head to look at Emma, and the night was slipping away. It seemed best to go over the wall without delay.

I squatted down and took hold of Emma. 'You have to stand up,' I whispered, 'and you must be silent.' As I spoke it occurred to me that sharp words might be better and I spoke to her harshly. 'Stand up and hold the fence and be still. Don't let me hear a sound. Do you hear?'

She looked at me, nodded docilely, and got up obediently and held onto the fence. Then she staggered me by saying, 'All right, Daniel.'

I half bent, ready to ask her if she truly recognised me, but checked myself and merely said, in as normal a voice as I could muster, 'Good girl'.

Very carefully I eased myself up and swung a leg over the fence. Everything stayed quiet. I pulled my other leg up and began to lower myself. As I did so a deep growl came from the darkness. It was Cranley's dog. The growl came again, coarse and menacing. 'Good boy,' I whispered, 'good lad. Get back now. Down.'

In its brutish way the dog recognised my voice and its growl died away. I lowered myself from the fence and, when I was down, made little chucking noises, hoping to draw the dog to me.

I thought that if I could grab it I might choke it. The dog did not growl again but backed away into the light. There it sat down and wagged its tail. Although this was an improvement on the growl I did not care to think what Cranley would make of it if he looked out of the window and saw his dog wagging its tail at the darkness.

However it was quiet, so I turned back to the fence. There was some rubbish piled in the angle where the fence met the wall. I stood on this, walking as gently as though I were walking on egg-shells, and muttered to Emma to hold her arms up. To my relief she did this without a murmur and I lifted her easily. We made no noise for the rubbish under our feet was old cloth, but with Emma's weight as well as mine it gave beneath us. As it settled a dark shape flicked from it. It was a rat.

CHAPTER TWENTY

The dog spotted the rat, jumped at it, and burst into a savage raucous barking. I wasted no time. I dragged Emma to the gate and threw back the top bolt. But as I stooped to draw the bottom one a light fell full on me. I heard a shout and saw Cranley framed in the door. I dashed back the bolt, seized Emma by the hand, and ran.

I made to go to my left, to dodge around the mill, but I heard a shout and saw a dark figure, a sentry. I changed my direction in mid-stride and made for the Clough. I had Emma's hand in mine and she ran as fleetly as I did but stiffly, as though she were some kind of machine running to order. But however she ran she was with me when we reached the brook. I had it in mind to cross and lose our pursuers in the woods but there was no possibility of that. The water boiled among the rocks in such a way as would have given an otter pause. Behind us I heard Cranley shout. There was only one way for us. I took it and headed upwards.

The way was familiar to me, I had been up it hundreds of times. But then I had been able to go as I pleased, picking my way along the narrow path, between the steep bank on one side and the sheer drop into the brook on the other. Now, pursued, in the moonlight, with Emma hanging onto my arm, and a rope waiting for my neck if I was caught, it was another matter. We had to make what haste we could. The path was slippery with mud and the hawthorns clawed at us as we threaded our way among them. Our salvation was that our chasers had to go as slowly as we did and we, being smaller and lighter than they, had the advantage.

But going so slowly made the chase a weird one. Our progress was almost leisurely and it was hard not to think that we could, if we wished, rest ourselves. The moon was full out and the Clough was flooded with a clear silvery light. Now and then I looked backwards and saw a dark hunched figure scuttling through the bushes. It was Cranley, his cut was unmistakable. I could see no other men.

We were near the head of the Clough now. I called on Emma to hurry, but whether she heard me or not I do not know. It was hard to hear above the noise of the water. It poured over the sluice in a huge, glassy sheet and when it hit the rocks below gave off a vast, throbbing 'Boom!' which echoed across the cleft. The air was dense with spray thrown up by the force of the fall. The trees and rocks, and we ourselves, were so saturated with water that it became hard to move. But we struggled on a little, and a little further—then I slipped and fell.

I went down awkwardly and felt a stabbing pain in my ankle. I tried to get up but only managed to hurt my leg more. I waved

Emma on but she did not go. Instead she bent over me and tugged at my coat.

'Run, Daniel,' she cried in a high piping voice which carried over the dull roar of the stream. 'Run, Daniel. The man will get you. The man will beat you. Run Daniel. Run Daniel.'

She was still calling on me to run when Cranley came upon us.

At first I thought that we had been overlooked for he took a pace past us. But the dog, following on his heels, stopped dead and growled. Cranley stopped too, turned on his heel, and stared down. His face was lost in shadow but I knew what inhuman lineaments of brutality were written there. He carried a stick and he shook it over his head as if in triumph. I pulled Emma to me in a gesture of protection.

'That's the man,' she cried, and again, 'that's the man.'

And indeed it was the man; squat, enduring, triumphant, and wearing his old hat like a laurel crown. In a futile act of defiance I scraped some mud from the path and threw it at him. It spattered on his breeches. In return Cranley kicked me, not hard. He was, I thought, measuring his distance but before he could kick again there came a vivid orange flash and a bang and Cranley lurched sideways. He did not fall but as he recovered himself a lank figure hurled itself from the darkness and smashed into him. Cranley disappeared as if the earth had swallowed him and there, in his stead, capering on the brink of the Clough, waving a musket, and screaming a high-pitched scream, was Briggs!

I stared at the apparition, dumb-struck. Then he turned and saw me. He waved his musket in the air and I was afraid that I was due to follow Cranley down the Clough. 'Briggs!' I bellowed. He paused and cocked his head. I shouted his name again. I suppose that something in the darkness of his mind recognised my voice and that the recognition frightened him, for he threw down the musket and ran off up the Clough.

He ran off and I lost sight of him for a moment. When I saw him again he was on the sluice. At first I could not make out what he was doing for he seemed to be bending and stooping then straightening himself again. It took me some little time to realise that he was hacking at the sluice with an axe. I raised my arms in protest, then let them fall. Let the sluice go. It would damage the mill to be sure. At least the children would have a rest. I turned away determined to grasp the chance the hour had brought and to drag myself and Emma away. But as I turned I saw Cranley.

At first I doubted my eyes. I had thought that when Briggs had knocked him in the Clough he had gone for ever, yet here he was, hooking his fingers through the thin earth to the rock and dragging himself from the abyss. I found myself moving across the path and I threw out my hand to Cranley to aid him. Cranley's hat had gone and I could see his face clearly. His eyes were quite fixed on mine. Whether he saw me or not I do not know. But as our finger-tips brushed he seized my wrist. To this day I do not know whether he intended to pull himself up—or me down with him. But his grip was slack and his fingers slipped from my hand. And then I became aware of something else. The noise of the water was changing. Before it had dashed onto the rocks in a raving kind of way but now there was a steadier tone, almost lazy or lethargic. It was more frightening than before. It had a fearsome note of power, an inevitable strength that seemed to shake the Clough. From the cleft a white mist rose, covering the rocks and trees, until it lapped at the sluice itself and all that was visible was the black line of the timbers and Briggs' phantasmal figure perched on them.

Briggs was not capering now. He was perfectly still, his head cocked as if he was listening, enraptured, to the voice of the water, or seeing in the mist some sight secret to all the world but him. And as he stood entranced, the timbers moved slowly. I thought I heard a scream, but that could have been the baulks of the sluice for they moved again, tilting over the chasm—and Cranley, and myself. I dared wait no longer but dragged myself away from the bank. As I did so Cranley seemed to nod at me. For sure he lifted his hand, but whether it was a plea for help, to bid me farewell, or to strike a last blow, I cannot tell. Then there was an enormous 'Boom!' and a vast white wave broke through the sluice. As it rushed out it threw black shapes high in the air. And one of them twisted as it arced across the sky and seemed to snatch at the stars before it, too, was lost in the coiling mist.

The deluge lasted no more than a minute. When it had gone I went to the edge of the chasm. Cranley was no longer there.

I turned, stupefied, and hobbled back to Emma. I sat by her and held her in my arms. From far away we heard a noise like distant thunder, a sullen, throbbing thud as the wave smote the mill, and then all was quiet. The gurgle of the water of the lodge died away as it emptied and there was only the gentle tinkle of the stream and the plaintive cry of some night bird.

We were still there, crouched against each other, when Luke came a-hunting for us. Emma was asleep and did not waken when Luke picked her up. I, myself, was close to the edge of oblivion, but when Luke took me by the hand and led me forward I followed him. I followed him when he took me by the hand and led me from Fenner's Clough and over the moors to Spen. And not one creature stirred as we crossed the wilderness. Only the moon and the stars shone down on us as indifferently as though Cranley had never been, as if Briggs had never lived, and as if we, and our brief concerns, were of no more consequence than the slow beat of a moth's wing fluttering to the fire.

CHAPTER TWENTY-ONE

Bloom called on us yesterday. It is not the first time that he has made the journey over the moors to Spen in the past six years, but it seems it is to be his last.

I was astounded at his appearance. When we are young we get fixed notions of people, as if they are figures in a print and will stay that way for ever. So Bloom, to me, was always long and yellow, stooped, untidy, dressed in grey fustian and an old cap. But he appeared at our house in a smart coat of blue broadcloth, wearing green trousers and well polished shoes, and with a dapper grey hat on his head.

'Oi'm going home,' he announced. 'Moi Mum's getting on and she's ill, so oi'm going back to Brum to look after her.'

So Bloom had a mother! I stared at him in surprise. It had never occurred to me that he might have parents, and brothers and sisters, nephews and nieces, like any other man. He had always seemed to me more like a silent extension of a three-foot file.

'I'm going to work for Watt and B.' he said. 'I wrote, and they will give me a berth in the works at Soho. My Mum lives near there.'

He said this with the calmness of one whose future is assured, but there was no excitement in his voice, no fire glowed in his eyes when he spoke of Watt and B. as there had in the old days. He took off his hat and wiped his head. There was a red line where the hat had gripped his forehead. His hair started a long way back from it, and it was grey.

We had a meal together. Emma brought in bread and cheese and, in Bloom's honour, we mashed tea. We ate in silence.

Father spoke rarely these days and Luke, I knew, wished to save the talk until the table was cleared, and the candles lit, and the calm of the evening had come.

After the meal Bloom and I took a stroll down the valley. In his finery Bloom made a mild sensation in the villages and, had he not been with me who was well known in Spen, might well have been stoned.

The streets were thronged with people as ragged and wild looking as savages.

'Things look bad here,' Bloom said. 'How much do they get paid?'

'Tenpence a piece,' I answered. 'When they can get work.'

'What would that be a week?'

'About six shillings.'

'You couldn't keep a dog on that,' Bloom observed.

We strolled onto the bridge which crosses the Spen River and stared down at its dirty waters. Bloom looked at me sideways.

'You're all right, are you?' he asked.

I nodded. 'We have my wages, and Emma brings in a little.'

'We're lucky, being engineers.'

I could only agree with this. We turned from the bridge and walked back home. In Lee village we passed an inn. It was full of weavers, drunk to a man. There were women in there, and children too. I pointed at it.

'Six years ago a weavers' club used to meet there. It was called The Spen Weavers Improvement Society. They used to study Philosophy and Botany. It had four hundred members.'

'Aye?' Bloom shook his head. 'That was when all that marching was going on. I always said that it would come to no good.'

We walked home through the valley of degradation, back to our house. For an hour or two Bloom talked to Luke whose gentle face lit up as they talked of the night we took Emma from Cranley's mill.

'We will maybe strike some more blows for freedom before we are done,' said Luke. The candle-light shone in his eyes as he spoke and you would not have known that he was blind.

'Aye.' Bloom agreed, but it was plainly politeness and not conviction in his voice.

He stayed with us overnight, sharing Luke's bed. I stayed downstairs as usual, where I could aid my father should he need it.

This morning Bloom made his departure. He shook hands with Luke and father. Father had little to say. He lay in his bed, mute and withdrawn, his mind hemmed in by the cuts he got at Peterloo. Luke smiled his farewell:

'We may meet again. Perhaps we will call on you in Birmingham when we go down to Parliament.'

'Oh, and will you be going to Parliament then?' Bloom asked.

'Maybe. Times might change for the better for us.'

'Well you're right for a bed in Brum if you get that way.'

Bloom meant the offer, I am sure, but it was clear he did not expect that it would ever be taken up.

It being Sunday I offered to walk Bloom on his way and nothing would do Emma but that she must come too. We walked across the moors to Todmorden. Bloom asked me whether Luke was serious in talking about going to Parliament.

'I thought all that had been knocked out of the weavers' heads,' he said. 'What good comes of it? You will have the magistrates down on you for sure.'

'I think not,' I said. 'Have you not heard? The Six Acts are repealed as from tomorrow.'

'Are they now?' Bloom looked thoughtful, as well he might for the Acts had hung over us since 1819, banning free speech and meetings.

'Yes. Now men may meet together and combine within the law. There is to be a procession in Spen next Saturday to celebrate it.'

It was my turn now to look sideways at Bloom. 'You saw the degradation of the weavers last night, but not all of us are so beaten down, you know.'

Bloom pursed his lips disapprovingly but made no further objections. I suppose he despaired of us.

On the brow of Constable Lee we parted. He shook my hand and ruffled Emma's hair.

'Why don't you come to Brum with me,' he asked. 'I could get you a job easily. Watt and B. would jump at a lad like you. Come on down, see a bit of civilisation.'

I shook my head. 'I wouldn't do it if I could. But thank you for the offer.'

'I didn't think you would come. Well—' Bloom looked about him. 'I doubt that we will meet again but I will write to you. Farewell.'

He turned on his heel and strode away. Just once he turned and raised his hand, and then I lost sight of him among the woods of Rawtenstall Clough.

And now it is evening. The wilderness in the east, Scout Hill and Rowley Moor, Noll Hill and Radley Head gathers the darkness to itself. The mist rises from the Irwell and spreads across the vale. Soon it will be hidden from sight and seem as it did when I was a lad. For it has changed. The moors still raise their monumental images but along their hems the houses cluster like black embroidery on a widow's weeds. When I used to work in Fenner's Clough I sometimes fancied that I could hear the looms chanting, 'For ever, for ever'. Now the chorus has been multiplied a thousand times and the hand-weavers of this vale have gone, almost as if they had never been. Almost. Those who were weavers, free men, but who are now enchained at their labours in the mills, they have not all forgotten the days of freedom. The memories last; rustless, imperishable, unfading. Let it be so. Our minds must feed on something or even our minds will die and we will all become no more than cattle, brute and dumb, mere beasts of burden.

Bloom listened patiently last night when Luke spoke of our days of glory. He is a kind man. But Luke's memories are not, as he thinks, the faded keepsakes of a withered mind. They are the seeds of our future.

A few lights are shining now. One of them twinkles from Helmshaw like a distant star. I have never been back there. When I wished to I dared not; now, when I may, I have no desire to. I could return. A man may walk on his own moor again without being harried by the magistrates. Have not the Six Acts been repealed? Indeed, I could have returned years ago. Fletcher sent for me to work in a mill he had built. There is a word for that; it is called irony. I like that word, irony. I use it now because I have learned many words since I marched down to Peterloo. It means, if I understand aright, that something is other than it seems. Surely that is true of the year of 1819. We thought that we would change the world, and the world has changed, but not as we intended it. When we were hacked down on St. Peter's fields the authorities thought that they were cutting out the shoot of freedom for ever. But what has happened? We had our martyrs, true: some died, some were hurt, grievously, Hunt and Bamford, and others too, lay in gaol for a time but now, while they are free as air and honoured for their lodging with the King, their enemies and ours are derided as villains and dare hardly show their faces on the public street.

And Cranley? There is the greatest irony of all. He was, I used to think, the wickedest man in the world and I hated him as my enemy and my father's enemy, which he was for sure. But what was he? In the end no more than an ignorant and squalid man who wrought his own destruction.

When I think of Cranley I think, as well, of another man. This man is Fielden and he too owns a mill. I tend his machines here in Spen. He is what you call a good man. His workmen are not ill-treated nor does he demand they grovel before him like dogs. And yet, like Cranley did, he uses machines. Like Cranley's they tire not and the hand-weavers go blind as they try to make their looms work as fast as the machinery.

And so I see this irony in Cranley and Fletcher and Fielden and all like them; good, bad, or indifferent, it makes no matter. Their machines know nothing of morality and, whoever is their master, like the god Moloch, they devour the infants placed before them.

Because of this I have no wish to see Fenner's Clough again. I know the mill moulders there, wrecked, weed-grown, silent, and somewhere beneath the rubble, under the broken walls, lie the bodies of Cranley and Briggs: but what happened there that night when we took Emma from its walls seems now no more than a fiction, a romance any pedlar will sell you for a farthing. There was nothing to learn from that night; the dull, laborious, uneventful years of Spen have taught me more.

It is time for us to go or night will catch us on the moors. Emma runs towards me, her arms full of flowers and her face bright with the rays of the setting sun. I put my book in my pocket. It was written by John Milton who was a blind poet in the time when a king's head rolled from under the people's axe. I bought it for three-farthing at Huddersfield market. The language is of the olden days and much of it I do not understand but there is one passage I like. This is what it says:

> 'Methinks I see in my mind a noble and puissant nation rousing herself like a strong man after sleep, and shaking her invincible locks. Methinks I see her as an eagle mewing her mighty youth and kindling her undazzled eyes at the full midday beam.'

Like Milton once as my father sat on the moor of Helmshaw he saw a vision. He saw black times coming for the weavers, he saw the day when the smoke of the chimneys would be their pall. His vision has come true but I, too, see a vision. I see the people of our valleys stretch their bent limbs and straighten their crooked backs, and rise like men, rise like their forefathers. I see that they will hammer out their destiny as I hammer out the black iron on the forge. It will be done in dirt and sweat; secretly, virtue mixed with vice, honesty with lies, nobility with treachery. And it will be done by them alone, not by men like Hunt and Fielden, be they never so good.

I see this as I look down on the dark vale, and I am not alone. There is a stirring in the land. Next Saturday we will march through Spen; not in our thousands as we marched to Peterloo, nor in our Sunday best, for we have none, but we will march. I told Bloom this and he shook his head in dismay. He would have shaken it off had I told him one thing more. We have a banner. It has no pretty true-love knots nor images of fair women. It is black and red and has no words embroidered on it but says, rather, in its blankness, make of me what you will. To be sure it is a grim ensign and fits our mood. And though not five dozen will march behind it I do not doubt that the hills will catch the echoes of our tread and, to be sure, millions not yet born will hear those echoes: and their minds will never cease from pondering their meaning.

And here are the names of the heroes of this book: George Cregg, weaver; James Adshead, weaver; Thomas Spencer, weaver; Sam Teller, weaver; Luke Simmons, weaver; Samuel Bamford, weaver; Obadiah Briggs, weaver; Henry Rowley, weaver; Tubal Bloom, engineer; John Giles, agitator; Joseph Healey, barber; Henry Hunt, gentleman; the weavers of the North to the number of one hundred thousand.

I do not write down the names of the villains.

'What is the price of experience? Do men
    buy it for a song?
Or wisdom for a dance in the streets? No it is
    bought with the price
Of all that a man hath, his house, his wife,
    his children.
Wisdom is sold in the desolate market where
    none come to buy,
And in the wither'd field where the farmer
    plows for bread in vain'.

William Blake.